# The Hunt for the Dingo

## Part One of the James & Sandersen Files
### P. J. Nash

www.bloodhoundbooks.com

Print ISBN : 978-1-912604-02-9

*WRITTEN BY
WANTON -
BASED
ACTION*

For Roary.

'Quis custiodet ipsos custodes?'
*Who shall guard the guards themselves?*
*Juvenal, Satire V1*

# Preface

## St Kilda, Melbourne, Australia.

The cold, steel-blue of an early dawn. Men swathed in bulky equipment mill around with exaggerated movements like latter-day mummies just escaped from the tomb. At 5am the first doors are going to go in.

You look around; all the guys are pretty lithe and fit. Even the guys gathered around in a knot smoking can do a 5k run in full gear. Different to your days in the Met, when being built like a brick shithouse was enough. These days, captor spray and batons can bring guys almost any size to their knees and make them cry like newborn babies. But if they're hopped up on meth and make a break for it, you've got a jog on. Not that it's too much of an issue, here, every officer is carrying at least one firearm, usually something of the nine-millimetre variety with a clip load of soft-nosed bullets. Hands cold with fear, you reach down and feel the reassuring weight of the Beretta in your shoulder holster.

Radios squawk. It's time to mount up. Cigarettes are discarded and ground out under heavy boot heels. The chatter dies down and helmets and balaclavas go on. "You're with us," a burly sergeant says, beckoning you to the nearest van which boasts the legend *Finnegan's Cake, Bakers*.

"You'll need this," another guy adds handing over a Kevlar vest with "Police" written in large white letters on the front and back.

"So you don't forget who you are," quips a wag from the murky interior of the van. The roller shutter door goes down and visibility is negligible.

What seems only seconds later, the door slams upwards and there is a collective shout of "Go, Go, Go!" The three men in front of you bomb-burst out of the truck. You follow, legs pumping, your heart pounding, a metallic tang cloying in your mouth. There is a cacophony of shouts and sounds of splintering wood and breaking glass. A series of bangs goes off and acrid smoke billows out of a doorway.

A hand reaches onto your shoulder and eagerly pushes you forward. "This way, sir," a friendly voice urges and suddenly you enter the smoky hallway, glass splintering under your boots as you pick your way up the narrow staircase.

You reach the top and turn. On the landing, what seems like a full-scale pitched battle is under way. A semi-naked man in his twenties is waving a meat cleaver, screaming obscenities like a staccato machine gun. A young woman, covered only with a hastily snatched up duvet, is also screaming and throwing stuff. Two officers have drawn their weapons, and another has his captor spray, ready to take down the cleaver man. There's no room to manoeuvre, so you back down the stairs, hand reaching for your weapon.

Footsteps clump down the stairs and you turn, expecting to see a fellow officer. But it's not, it's him. "Morning, copper," he says, levelling a nickel-plated handgun at you. A cry begins to form in your mouth but nothing happens. There is a flash of light and a burst of heat…

\*\*\*

Lawrence James sat bolt upright in bed. He was covered in sweat. It had been the same dream from that same day that had plagued him for the last few months. Bugger knows how he could shake the dream off, but he knew that putting Cyrus Bain away for a *very* long time would certainly be a good start.

# Stuart Highway, Northern Territory, Australia.

The Stuart Highway runs a thousand miles across an endless horizon from Alice Springs in the Red Centre to Darwin on the tropical coast. The road splits the Northern Territory in two and progresses across the moon-like interior, interrupted only by the occasional truck stop or small town.

It was this two-lane road that was the beat of Constable Dan Collins of the Northern Territory Police. Collins was gunning the police Ford Falcon down the blacktop at top speed as his colleague Allan "Toohey" Campbell loaded shells into his 12-gauge shotgun. Nicknamed for his fondness for Toohey's beer, he had been riding two-up with Collins for the past three years. The day had started off quietly enough with a chance to catch up with some long overdue crime records. But things had changed when Bob "The Beast" Clarke had turned up in town. This could only mean one thing: mayhem.

"Suppose the bugger was going to kick off at some point," shouted Toohey over the blaring siren.

"You should have chucked your five bucks in yesterday. The odds have got to be better than the pokies," said Collins, without moving his eyes from the road.

"Here we go, show time," said Toohey, as the Patterson place appeared on the right of the Highway. Collins braked hard and swung the car off the road and on to the rutted and pot-holed track. The speeding car raised a plume of red dust as it bounced and jerked over the rough terrain. The two officers had been scrambled to respond to an emergency call made by Clarke's terrified daughter.

"Dad's done his nut! He said he saw someone in the sheds and he's gone down there with the shotgun," she'd screamed.

Collins swerved the car to a halt. Both men got out, keeping low as they did. Toohey signalled that he would circle around the straggle of buildings. Collins un-holstered his Glock 22 .40cal pistol and made for what appeared to be the front of the place. Bob "The Beast" Clarke, six feet five tall and weighing in at twenty-five stones, all tattoo-covered muscle, would make his presence felt two or three times a year. Normally he worked away, mining for opals in Mount Isa, but every few months he would arrive in town like a horseman of the apocalypse to drink and gamble away his wages, and harangue his long-suffering wife, Jean. Somewhere within the first forty-eight hours, Collins or one of his colleagues would get the call. When news arrived he was in town, bets were taken amongst the cops as to just when Clarke would kick off.

A shotgun boomed and there was a sound of breaking glass from nearby. Using the cover of a rusting pickup, Collins made his way across the gap between two ramshackle sheds. Peering cautiously around the corner, he saw Toohey confronting Clarke.

"Put the gun down, Bob, we'll take care of your prowler," said Toohey, calmly.

"Fuck off copper, you just want to take me in," Clarke spat back.

Toohey saw Collins emerge quietly from the corner of the shed. He also saw the other officer make a twin V-shape with his fingers outwards. With just the slightest twitch of his head Toohey nodded his assent and worked out that he needed to buy a few moments.

"Okay, look here, Bob, I'm going to put my gun down and then we can just talk like two regular guys, okay?" said Toohey placing the shotgun down in the dust and then stepping back.

"Well, I'm keeping mine, pig," said Clarke, waving the shotgun in Toohey's direction.

The ruse had worked. Collins was back.

"Okay Bob, I'm going ask you to put the gun down, and then if you don't, I'm going to have to withdraw my offer? Get it?"

"Fuck you, copper," said Clarke, reversing the gun and charging towards Toohey.

When a Taser is deployed there is no blue flash. There is a reasonably loud pop or crack, the front gates of the cartridge fly off and the two barbed probes shoot forward and into the person being fired at. The two barbs both connect to the person being shot. The person experiences immediate incapacitation. They go very rigid and fall to the ground.

This is exactly what happened to Bob Clarke. He screamed uncontrollably. The whole thing took five seconds. Collins stood over Clarke. The barbs were still attached. If Clarke moved out of line, Collins could give him another five-second burst. But he was meek as a lamb.

In a well-rehearsed drill, Toohey had moved in as Clarke collapsed and slapped the handcuffs on him.

"I did tell you, Bob," said Toohey. "Don't think he likes our new toy, does he?"

The sound of a siren told the pair that backup was here. A marked police Hilux skidded to a halt and Constable Tom Johnson exited, his gun drawn.

"You can put the piece away," laughed Toohey, "This Beast is bagged ready for the cells."

"Okay, let's get him in the truck and the doc can give him a once over," said Johnson.

"I'll ride shotgun with Jonno and The Beast," said Toohey.

"Sure, I'll start taking some statements and take a look around see what all the palaver was about," said Collins.

With The Beast stowed safely aboard, Toohey and Johnson got in and drove off. Picking his way between a rusting Ford and a pile of indiscriminate scrap metal, Collins leant across to the passenger seat and picked up his clipboard. A sudden flash of movement told him something was wrong. He grabbed for his gun. A blow to the back of the head sent him crashing to the floor and everything went black...

# Safe-apartment, Melbourne, Australia.

Lawrence James was wishing he was having "just another day at the office". However, the cast on his arm and his boss had different ideas. He looked at his watch. It was another fifteen minutes before he would be able to take his first fix of co-codamol for the day. For someone who had spent many hours fighting the war on drugs, the irony was not lost on him. The drugs, in James' case, did work, fulfilling a dual role: Firstly, they stopped the majority of the pain from getting through and secondly, as one of his friends had ably surmised, "they rounded all the sharp edges" that one faced in daily life.

It was the drugs and a rigidly adhered to routine that had kept James from going stir-crazy over the past few weeks. The dinging bell of a tram making its stately progress up the slope of Swanston Street reminded James that Melbourne was waking up to a new morning.

Commuters would be clutching their cappuccinos and their raincoats, equipped with caffeine and the essential piece of clothing that allowed them to cope with the city that had given rise to the term "four seasons in one day". James no longer felt part of that world. His world had been reduced to the microcosm of this two-bedroom apartment; the city had been distilled into what he could garner from phone calls, texts from colleagues and his daily copy of *The Age*, of which he devoured every inch.

Even this fragile lifeline had nearly been severed after an overzealous delivery boy had knocked too hard. He had been jolted from his adolescent daze when the door was whipped open and a .38 Special Smith & Wesson revolver was thrust under his chin.

A stab of pain through his arm brought James back to the frustrating immediacy of the predicament and the events leading to his "voluntary" incarceration. To put it plainly, he had taken a bullet in the arm whilst leading a door entry team on a raid on a crack house.

His role as Intelligence Liaison Officer from the Serious Crimes Squad was to visually identify Cyrus Bain. James and the Serious Crimes Squad had got the inside dope on Bain, but the Commissioner was keen to let the uniform boys take the collar. As James had pointed out at the time, the story that Bain had been taken alive by the uniform boys also helped to put a dent in his previously undisputed reputation as the leader of the infamous Redbacks, a gang who were conservatively estimated to be responsible for sixty per cent of the hard drugs supply in the Melbourne metropolitan area, along with the associated murders, shootings and beatings that came with it. The Redbacks were not so much a gang, but more of a franchise that allowed loose affiliates of gangs to do business together. Bain, however, had, by the dollar and the gun, brought these loose affiliates together through a series of "mergers and acquisitions" which instead of ending in executive bonuses, led to bodies in the Yarra River.

The cops in Melbourne had been trying to nail Bain for nearly a decade. But Bain was a smart cookie. His organisation wasn't hierarchical. It was cellular. The people in their cell only know their immediate contacts. So if a cell was lost, the organisation remained unaffected. It also made the planting of undercover cops nigh on impossible and scarcely worth it, given the risks involved.

James had done their job for them, in a few fleeting seconds as he had stood, the only thing between Bain and freedom. The fleeing gangster had calmly taken aim, fired a shot that he knew would wound, not kill, and stepped calmly over the prostrate James. He'd paused to light a cigarette and throw his jacket into a skip. Unfortunately for him, he hadn't spotted the uniform cop taking a brief pause from his duties on cordon duty, in support of the raid. The cop had been relieving himself on the other side of the skip when he recognised the black-clad figure of Bain, whose description had just been broadcast over the radio net. Promptly whacking the distracted Bain with his baton, the cop had cuffed him.

Bain was triumphantly brought up the steps of police headquarters in front of a full cohort of the city's press.

The next morning, while Bain was being brought before a magistrate on a charge of attempted murder, James was being lauded in the media as a wounded hero. He made the front page of the newspapers and the top of the Redbacks' death list. Dislocating the livelihoods of several thousand scumbags, from the top-level players to the street-level pushers, made you enemies fast. A uniformed cop had stood guard outside James' room around the clock. But when a medical orderly carrying a tray bearing a syringe full of the Redbacks' finest street product was challenged at the entrance to the wing by a civilian security guard, it was time to move James underground.

And so here he was in a studio flat tucked away from harm and missing his girlfriend, Monica, who had been whisked away to an unknown destination. Cut off from the world, with only the ever-present prospect of death hovering, and not even a latte to keep him company.

# Chandler Hospital, Chandler, Northern Territory.

Collins woke to a piercing light in his eyes. It belonged to a doctor's flashlight, in a ward of Chandler Hospital. Old man Patterson had found him lying in the red dust. He'd been out cold for a few minutes. Collins blinked and saw the familiar face of his commander, Jez Wexford, standing over his bed.

"You're a lucky bastard, I heard he knocked some sense *into* you?" guffawed Wexford.

"Something like that," said Collins, not quite ready to face the bonhomie of his commander.

"Whoever jumped you knew what they were doing," said the doctor pocketing his flashlight.

"How so?" asked Collins.

"Well, the scans come up free and clear as regards to any damage to your skull, yet you received a hell of a blow that put you out for a good while. That takes practice," the doctor said, with too much relish for someone whose profession was apparently healing, not hurting.

"Balls, he just lashed out at Dan here," Wexford said, waving a dismissive hand before returning it to his belt to hoist his trousers around his corpulent waistline.

"You found anything out at the Patterson place?" asked Collins, whose skull, the subject of the conversation, now began throbbing just enough for him to put an end to this bedside conference.

"Not really, just some clothes and other crap that the guy had been using. He'd been crashing in one of the Patterson's old sheds," said Wexford, scratching his jowly chin. "I put the wind up old man Patterson and told him if he was planning to play host to any more guests who assault my officers I'd be back with a full search warrant and a man from the tax office. That seemed to do the trick," chortled Wexford, obviously pleased with his big man act.

"So you got the clothes to forensics, see if we can check for known criminals?" asked Collins.

"Don't be such a wet fart, this isn't bloody CGI New York," spat Wexford contemptuously, showing his ignorance of both basic police procedure and contemporary US crime drama. Going red in the face, he wasn't finished quite yet. "You got jumped by some drifter, not fucking Moriarty," blustered Wexford. "I gave 'em old man Patterson and told him to burn them. Anyway, old son, you rest up for a day or two and make sure your bonce is back in order before you come back, eh?"

With this, he waddled out of the room. The doctor replaced the clipboard at the bottom of Collin's bed, mumbled something about "too many cops" and left. Barely had the doctor left the room and Collin's thoughts began to turn to the prospect of sleep, than the well-polished boots of Toohey strode in.

"Hi, I heard you took a thumping?" said Toohey, leaning his six foot six inches frame over the bed. "What happened?"

"Not the foggiest, mate. I was just out in the car and then a shadow went across my back and the lights went out," said Collins.

"Like the doc said then, a pro," added Toohey.

"I reckon so, too," said Collins as he left his sleep-like state and emerged into full wakefulness.

"Put it like this, if it was a drifter, why would he take a pop at you and risk an assault charge? It's not like you were poking around the place, all they'd have needed to do is not move and you'd have been gone."

"Well, we'll never know, now that arsehole got rid of all the evidence. But you're right: it feels like someone was spooked and had something big to hide," said Collins.

"Agreed," said Toohey. "I reckon we're going to take another look around the Patterson place."

"Okay man, see what you can find out, but be careful," said Collins, feeling nauseous as the painkillers ceased doing their work.

Toohey said his goodbyes and left Collins to get some well-deserved rest.

# The Patterson place, Northern Territory, Australia.

Toohey peered through the dirty glass of a window in the first shack that made up the outlying buildings of the Patterson homestead. He had returned with a warrant. After listening carefully for a minute or so he made for the front of the ramshackle building. Holding his shotgun forward he kicked the flimsy wooden door in. Satisfied no one was lurking in the interior, he went inside. The floor was scattered with rusting farm implements and bits of broken glass. He put the safety catch of the shotgun on and tucked the firearm under one arm. With his free hand he unhooked a Maglite torch from his belt, switched it on and played the bright beam across the interior of the shed.

He kicked aside rusting cans and probed the piles of garbage with the butt of the gun, but nothing caught his eye as unduly strange. Turning on his heel he went to go out of the door, tripping over a concealed chain as he did so.

"Oh, you bastard!" he cursed, just about stopping himself from crashing back out through the doorway. With his free hand he pulled the chain as hard as he could with all the force he could muster. But it didn't yield an inch. He put the shotgun down on the floor and pulled the chain with both hands. Garbage fell from the pile at the edge of the room and the chain moved several feet through his hands and snagged on something. Realising brute force wasn't getting him anywhere, Toohey followed the chain link by link until it disappeared into a pile of rags. He soon found that the pile of rags hid a large agricultural fertiliser bag.

He pulled on the last visible link of chain and then the sack moved across the floor, heavy with some unknown contents. Pushing the door fully open to get more light, Toohey looked back into the shack and saw that the chain was wrapped around a pair of well-manicured female feet, the rest thankfully hidden by the plastic fertiliser sack.

# Safe-apartment, Melbourne.

James was in the microscopic kitchen of his flat when his untraceable, cheap, pay-as-you go mobile phone beeped. He put down the coffee chair and picked up the phone and read the message which simply said, "Pack your shorts; you're off to the NT."

# Northern Territory Police HQ, Darwin, Northern Territory.

At 18.00 Central Standard Time the Northern Territory Police held a brief press conference. A press officer stood up and announced: "On Wednesday afternoon, at 3.25pm, one of our officers, conducting a routine search relating to a previous assault on one of our officers, discovered the body of a young British woman, who has now been identified as Kirsty Jessop, aged 18, from the UK. Her body was discovered in a disused building several miles east of the Tamworth Roadhouse. A major investigation has been launched and detectives are attempting to put together Kirsty's last known movements before her death.

We are appealing for any witnesses who may have been in the vicinity of the Tamworth Roadhouse in the past seventy-two hours to come forward. Anyone with information is asked to call the Incident Room in Darwin. We will be holding a press conference tomorrow morning here at 10am to further update you and when we will be able to answer questions. Thank you."

And with that the press conference was over, the spokesman disappeared and the assembled journalists filed rapidly out of the room to relay the bare facts they had been offered. They would fill the gaps with speculation and supposition.

# Somewhere between Melbourne & Darwin.

As the interstate coach ploughed through the night, James, confident he was not being tailed, removed his baseball cap and reached into his leather holdall. Nestling underneath a .38 Special was a dull brown foolscap folder held tightly shut, which he took out. He removed the elastic bands and began to read. What the spokesman had not told the assembled ladies and gentlemen of the press was that a DNA swab from the scene of the crime had been matched to one already found on the national database. The DNA match and the mode of death had triggered an alert at Victoria State Police. The DNA sample had been rushed through and confirmed the worst fears of some of the older detectives who had forsaken a night at home with their families, wives or girlfriends to hear the preliminary results. After lying dormant for over five years The Dingo Case had become live again.

# Dingo Killer Taunts Police over Fourth Victim

*A**lice Springs: Northern Territory Police are being taunted by a serial killer who has been dubbed "The Dingo" in law enforcement circles, it has been reported. The killer, whose fourth victim is a twenty-two-year-old British tourist as yet unnamed, has sent a series of type-written notes to detectives leading the investigation at the police headquarters in Darwin.*

James turned over the page of the photocopied newspaper article and read the supplementary handwritten notes. He had been reading steadily for the past two hours by the light of his torch.

Over the low hum of the air-conditioning which cocooned him and his fellow passengers from the reality of the blistering heat outside, James could hear snores and the tinny beat of an MP3 player being played too loudly. *Rusty*, thought James, running through the mental map he had of his fellow passengers. Rusty was the name he had badged the teenager three rows of seats back on the righthand side of the coach. One row after Jim and Mabel, a couple in their fifties; and in front of him, The Mullet King, a lean tattooed man in his thirties sporting a leather waistcoat and a fine example of a closely cropped pate with long flowing hair to the rear.

On the way to and from his bathroom break, during which he had texted his superiors back in Melbourne, James had felt an initial pang of concern about The Mullet King. This fear quickly dissipated though, for two reasons. Firstly, even the most inept gangsters (which the Redbacks were far from being) would not send an assassin in such an obvious manner. Secondly, the tattoos he sported were not gang affiliated, and were far too professionally done for prison efforts. After working closely amongst inner city gangs, James read tattoos like an entomologist reads the markings of a moth or butterfly.

While his fellow passengers slept on and the coach rolled up a few more kilometres, James selected the next photocopied sheet and read on.

*** 

Unbeknownst to James, Jim and Mabel were more lethal than first appearances would grant. Jim was retired Constable Bill Matthews and Mabel was a heavily made-up Constable Jenson. Both carried .38 Police Special revolvers, and were acting as guardian angels for James. They were the relief crew for Constable Nick Cross – aka The Mullet King – who had been on the coach with James since Melbourne. Nick would be losing his hair extensions before he returned to his more mundane police duties, but would be keeping the .38 Police Special strapped inside his leather waistcoat.

If Rusty had known how many cops were on the coach he would have been more than a little concerned about the two ounces of Moroccan Black hashish he had stashed in the hollowed out soles of his Dr. Martens boots. The driver nosed the coach forward at a steady sixty kilometres an hour towards the first fingers of light which heralded the start of a new day.

James leafed through another sheaf of clippings and their crime report counterparts. Truth be told, the coverage and the crime reports quickly merged into one, and rather than helping him build a coherent picture, it gave a distorted view of what had happened.

The Dingo murders had been committed over a thirty-month spree during the late 1990s and had suddenly stopped in the winter of 2000. The killer had claimed four definite victims over the time frame. His victims had all been young, attractive women.

All were from the UK and all had been visiting Australia as part of a round the world trip, usually on daddy's gold card. All had been mutilated in some manner before being strangled or stabbed. All the bodies had been dumped in outhouses or abandoned buildings where the killer had probably known the body would be found within a few days. The Northern Territory summer heat soon gets to work on a body.

The Dingo had been given his moniker after three bodies in a row had been found by ranchers out shooting dingoes who had been feeding on cattle carcasses, only to discover the desiccated corpse of a young woman. The tag had also stuck for the manner in the way in which the killer had selected easy targets in the shape of naïve women on their own in a strange country, reminiscent of the manner of a dingo carrying off calves.

The fact that the case stemmed from the late nineties struck James as he looked again at the sheaf of newspaper clippings and paper-based reports. These were the days of inky-fingered journalists, hot metal presses and long, liquid lunches. Among the hyperbole of the many journalists all nursing their pet theories about The Dingo, only one journalist stood out as having any objectivity and depth of analysis, at least in James' opinion.

His name was Adrian Marsh, the crime correspondent of the now defunct newspaper *The Darwin Telegraph*, nicknamed "The Bush" after the bush telegraph. He had covered the whole case until it finally fizzled out in the winter of 2000. James made a mental note to chase the guy up, hoping he hadn't drunk himself into an early grave.

Missing from the repertoire of people who inevitably crowd around the phenomenon of a serial killer were the plethora of psychologists and shrinks who offered their cod theories about disturbed childhood this and paranoid fantasist that. In the nineties, the ego of the journalists was sufficient to fill the column inches. In the ensuing years, however, a number of headshrinkers had trotted out books to supply the public's demand for true crime.

Reaching into his bag, James pulled out a thick hardback tome, entitled *On the Trail of the Dingo – a forensic psychologist's assessment of Australia's most notorious unsolved serial killer* by Dr Jessie Sandersen of Melbourne University. Tired of reading the ramblings and suppositions of journalists, James thought he'd take a look at the view from the lofty heights of academia. He flicked the book open and took in the carefully posed "I'm serious, but sexy" picture of the good doctor on the flyleaf of the book.

"Not bad at all," murmured James to no one in particular, the allure of the female preppy academic briefly interrupting the tawdry monotony of the whir of the air-conditioning and the tinny sounds emanating from Rusty's headphones.

James had crossed swords with Dr Sandersen previously on several occasions. Usually Sandersen followed James into the witness box as an expert witness for the defence to try and explain how a traumatic childhood or being bullied at school has caused criminal A to be caught in a house full of crystal meth with an illegal handgun shoved in their waistband or why criminal X's low self-esteem had caused him to remove the fingernails or teeth of a rival gang member with a pair of pliers. As a consequence, James had a slightly different opinion of Dr Sandersen than the sycophantic copy on the blurb of the book, which called her "One of Australia's most talented and insightful psychologists".

"Most accomplished at making the psychological background fit the excuse for the crime," mumbled James to himself. His temporary swirl of resentment subsided and the nullifying tiredness that comes from the sedentary nature of long distance travel swept over him and he was soon asleep. The tinny noise emanating from Rusty's MP3 player had taken a more relaxed note as he moved from Pink Floyd to Nick Drake for the journey through the night.

# Chandler, Northern Territory.

Thanks to being whacked over the head by an unknown assailant, Dan Collins had been put on light duties for three days. This meant he had to spend most of his time in and around the vicinity of Chandler Police Station. It wasn't long before he was wishing for the crisp white sheets and the tender loving care from the nurses which only those wounded in the line of duty deserve to receive.

The IT monkeys were in that morning, running in cables and fumbling with routers and all sorts of equipment. Despite the paraphernalia of modern technology, the murder board, which stood in the middle of the room, bore the picture of the fresh-faced Kirsty Jessop smiling out of a group photo, taken in Sydney only a few days before. The picture which had been issued to the press bore little resemblance to the gruesome pictures which were displayed lower down on the board and were most definitely *not* for public consumption.

Then, from on high, orders came to Collins that made him feel like a character in a cheap dime thriller. In the heat of the early afternoon, he found himself standing in a phone kiosk at the bus station, watching passengers stepping off the coach. He noted a man whose non-descript clothes screamed "copper" to his trained eye. And now, to make him feel even more like a character in a thriller, the phone by his elbow jangled into life, and he knew he was in business. He picked up the receiver.

"Is that Wayne?" a voice asked.

"Wayne's not here, but Dan is," Collins replied.

Replacing the receiver, he made his way along the street to The Rice Bowl. A few minutes later he was sitting alone at the bar when a man in his late thirties approached him, his left arm in a light cast.

"Mr Collins?" the man asked.

"Yes, that's me."

The man took the stool next to Dan. "I've come about the pest problem, a dingo, I believe?"

Collins could tell from the cheeky glint behind the brown eyes that he and James would get along. He also knew that there was a lot of ground to cover and that time was of the essence. But that time would come tomorrow over the tasteless, watery coffee and curling sandwiches of the Incident Control Room. Now was the time for spring rolls, dumplings, duck, egg fried rice and a couple of cold ones.

# Supermax, HM Prison Barwon,
# Nr Geelong, Victoria.

In less salubrious surroundings two other men were conducting a little business of their own. Paradoxically they were planning someone's demise rather than trying to prevent further ones. Many films depict the subtle manners and codes that allow incarcerated criminals, their lawyers, and associates to communicate. Cyrus Bain had simply sent a postcard to the head prison guard of his section. The postcard had shown a giggly young girl being pushed in a swing by an adoring mother and the legend "Greetings from Perth" on it. On the rear a mobile phone number had been printed. The prison guard had dialled it.

A voice said, "Great looking wifey you got there and a ripper of a little kid, too. Mr Bain will be visited by his lawyer at 2pm tomorrow. He'd appreciate some free time with his lawyer. There won't be any problems with that will there?"

"N…no, indeed not, 2pm is fine," the prison guard had said, attempting to maintain his composure.

The line had gone dead. Perth might have been several thousand miles away, but not far enough.

"Cigar?" Cyrus Bain asked, pushing a hand-tooled leather cigar case across the scratched Formica-topped table. The case was a rare piece of quality craftsmanship, which stood out in marked contrast to the bolted down furniture and barred window in the spartan setting of the room. Cyrus Bain, thirty-eight and career criminal since stealing his first car at sixteen to celebrate his exams, was not your archetypal gangster. At just under six feet and neither svelte nor fat, he boasted no tattoos nor skinhead haircut. He did, however, possess a certain feline grace and had an economy of movement. His green eyes burned with a keen energy which suggested he was always mentally engaged, despite giving an outward expression of languidness.

"So who's the pest that needs eradicating?" said Bain, extracting a Montecristo Number 2 from the case and expertly nipping off the end with a cutter. The end shot onto the floor where it settled. It would be swept up later by one of Bain's minions – a fellow Redback. It was against prison policy for gang members to be held on the same wing, as much as it was for inmates to meet with lawyers in private, or, indeed, smoke, but Bain had made his own rules during his incarceration.

"This is the toerag," said Curtis Howard, pushing a fat manila folder over to Bain who pulled the ten by eight-inch colour photograph of a male in his mid-thirties looking morosely out of an upstairs window. The picture had been taken through a telephoto lens but the image quality was good. Bain could read the Victoria Police logo on the man's t-shirt.

"That's one Lawrence James. A Pommie who started out in the Brit Met but came over following a skirt. He joined CID and then worked the Armed Offenders Squad for three years – he managed to avoid the fall-out and keep his badge, seemed he had kept himself squeaky clean – he was under surveillance for two weeks – that's where this shot was taken."

"Where do you get these?" asked Howard, picking up the cigar case.

"Well, let's say I'm paying two lots of school fees," said Bain laconically.

"Taking down a blue-boy is going to cost some serious bongo," said Howard. "And not your average gun and go, either," he added.

"It's taken care of already," said Bain striking a match and rolling the Cuban cigar around in his hand through the flame to get an even light.

"I'm getting a buy one, get one free deal," laughed Bain taking a pull on the Montecristo and enjoying the complex taste of the hot smoke. "So what's your little weasel got for us," he asked, exhaling a plume of blue cigar smoke towards the ceiling.

"James left town on a coach bound for the NT last night," said Howard.

"Okay, pass the details to Monty and let him know the whereabouts of the weasel. He's squeaked for the last time," said Bain.

"No worries, we'll sort it ASAP," said Howard putting some papers back into his case and exiting the cell. Visiting the jail made him uneasy and some of his lawyer friends shunned him, but as he settled into the leather driver's seat of his five series BMW, with plans for a swim followed by a massage, his reputation in the Melbourne law community slipped easily from his mind.

# Chandler, Northern Territory.

Relaxing amongst the debris of their meal the two men sat back, their appetites sated. Collins motioned to the young Chinese waitress, "Two more beers here, please, love," he said.

"So I know all the cloak and dagger stuff's off limits to a flat foot like me, but surely you can tell me a bit about how a Pom like you washes up in one-horse town like this on the other side of the world?" said Collins, with a hint of irony.

"My stunning good looks and winning personality, I suppose – the Commissioner wants some eye candy in the Incident Room," said James in riposte.

"You're some kind of witch doctor, according to the word around the camp-fire," said Collins.

"You've heard of the Butcher of Balham, right?" said James expecting a blank face.

"Operation Mercury, you mean?" said Collins with a wry smile, now not regretting spending several hours the previous evening reading James' file whilst fending off his wife's efforts to get him to fix the storm screens on the house.

"The very same," said James, giving a quiet nod of appreciation to the waitress who had returned with the two beers, which she carefully placed in front of them.

"Fancy a proper drink? I've had enough of this pop and I get to claim expenses," said Collins with a conspiratorial look.

"Sure, why not."

"Can we have the shooter menu, please, darling," said Collins, winking at the waitress, who nodded and swept gracefully to the bar.

"I was a detective sergeant in the Metropolitan Police in London, looking for a fresh challenge after three years of busting up crack dens, when I got call from a Deputy Commander who was putting a team together."

"There'd been a series of murders, young foreign girls, mainly au pairs, right?" said Collins, helping himself to a handful of prawn crackers.

"That's right. He'd follow them from the tube station, wait till the family were asleep, break in and rape them," said James. "Until one night a girl put up a fight and he slit her throat," he said, pausing to take a pull on his beer.

"That's when his motive or his MO as your Brit cops on TV call it, changed, right?" asked Collins.

"He got a taste for blood after then and got more dangerous. Forgot about waiting for the families to go out and took the whole lot on. He'd tie them all up, rape the women, and then murder them wholesale," said James.

"But he never broke in, there was never any sign of forced entry, which gave you one bastard of a headache," said Collins.

"The bitch of all headaches! He murdered three families over two months, by which time the papers had got hold of it. Two of the incidents took place several streets apart in Balham – hence the Butcher tag," said James, "Which is when they formed the task force of headshrinkers and profilers," he added.

"And you," said Collins.

"I was just an extra body, who'd happened to have been on a little sojourn to Quantico to brush up my knowledge of serial killers," said James.

"Ah, the special relationship, eh? How's it feel to be a colonial?" said Collins.

"Like a very small fish in a very big pond," said James with a smile.

"And you came up with the honeytrap idea," said Collins.

"Good old Olena did, really. She was a twenty-five-year-old DC who'd been seconded to us from Interpol in Warsaw. We were bagging and tagging a family in Chelsea, when she said, 'He's a language teacher,'" said James.

"So you went back to all the priors and her theory added up," said Collins, a keen edge to his voice.

"Yes it tallied up, so we baited the trap. Olena and I went into deep cover. We even sent her back to Poland and got her to come back in through Heathrow so her back-story added up," James said.

"And you became a stockbroker in Chelsea with a posh wife and some kids to match," said Collins.

"The kids were my nephew and niece, to make sure there was a family resemblance, they enjoyed their 'new' house and private school," said James, with a smile.

"And you got the fox to the chicken coop pretty sharpish, didn't you?" said Collins, with an appreciative smile.

"Two weeks and three days later Campbell Urquhart was sitting in our living room, when I reached behind the chair I was sitting in, pulled out my captor spray, gave him a healthy dose and Olena cuffed him," said James with obvious pride in his voice.

"His digital camera was full of images of me, her and the kids. When we took his bedsit apart he'd got details of three other families and plenty of 'trophies' from the previous attacks."

"So a job well done and a monster in a cage where he belonged?" said Collins.

"Well so it would have seemed, if it wasn't for that little word called 'entrapment' and Howard Bingley QC," said James, a hint of bitterness tempering his previously jovial tone.

"He walked, didn't he, and you and Olena as the architects of the scheme were made the whipping boys for the media, while the suits upstairs washed their hands like Pontius fucking Pilate?" said Collins.

"Exactly," said James. "So I thought I'd beat it for a while and make a fresh start."

"And straight into a bullet from Cyrus Bain. Didn't they tell you the bad boys carry guns here?" said Collins, both men breaking into a laugh. "Urquhart the bastard got his just desserts anyway, didn't he, though?" asked Collins.

"They found him floating in the Thames with his dick in his mouth, and seventy per cent burns from a blow lamp. Let's just say the spectacularly clear CCTV footage of the guys dumping his body never got made public," said James. "Now what about these shooters? I thought you Aussies liked a drink?"

# Balmoral Hotel, Chandler, Northern Territory.

He wasn't sure if it was the Buzz Bomb or the Snakebite that had finally wiped him out, but Lawrence James was definitely feeling distinctly worse for wear as he fumbled for the key card to his room. Paying off the cab, he'd walked a few streets and then gone into a grog shop, picking up a six pack of Toohey's beer and some Marlboro Reds. Never a big smoker, James, like many "reformed" smokers, always fell off the wagon after a few beers.

Getting into his room, however, proved to be a little more difficult. Trying to hold the bag containing the beer whilst fishing in his pockets was taking all of his concentration. He heard the lift bell ping. Desperate to get into the safety of his room, he finally found the key card and slotted it into the door. He had just opened the door when the plastic bag split and the bottles of beer rolled like downed skittles across the corridor. As James scrabbled on the floor to pick them up, one came to rest against a perfectly manicured foot ensconced in a strappy high-heeled shoe. Following his line of sight up the well-toned leg, James made eye contact with an all too familiar face, that of Dr Jessie Sandersen.

"Good evening, Mr James? I see we're going to be neighbours," she said.

Immaculately dressed in a two-piece charcoal business suit and leaning on a small pull-along suitcase, the good doctor contrasted sharply with the rumpled man on his knees on the floor.

"Care for a cold one?" said James standing up and attempting some form of composure.

"Well that's probably the best offer I'm going to get in this one-horse town," said Sandersen, with a smile. "I'll let you get yourself together and give you a call in say half an hour," she said pulling her implacably small case into her room which had been opened for her by a fawning bell hop, who would, no doubt, dutifully bring up the rest of her plentiful luggage.

James picked up the remainder of his beers from the floor and gingerly made his way into his room. Collapsing on the bed, his resentment for Sandersen, for the fact that she had caught him looking like a clown and for the fact that she had been flown and had not had to sweat it out on the coach, burned for a while. But it soon fizzled to a dying ember when he thought of the figure she had cut as she had swept into her room and the sweet and unpatronising smile she had given him as he writhed on the floor. James couldn't help but admit he would be glad to be seeing more of her soon.

# Boxwood, Northern Territory.

S arah Knight was hot, flustered and had missed her ride out of town. So far the twenty-year-old fine art graduate's Australian trip had been more of an odyssey than the trip of a lifetime.

Being dumped by your boyfriend of three years, standing at a rain-sodden Melbourne tram stop, never leaves you in the best of moods.

She'd headed for Alice Springs, made a brief stop at Uluru and hooked up with two trustafarians who were driving up to the Top End to see the "real" Oz. A booze-fuelled three-day drive with the two men had done wonders for her self-esteem.

Finding a vacant parking spot with only some empty stubbies and a burnt-out roach had pointed to the fact that her services were no longer required. Ever open to taking a phlegmatic approach to life, Sarah decided to do what any self-respecting Brit abroad would do and headed for the bright lights.

The bright lights in Boxwood that night came to her in the form of the Moose Head Bar & Grill. Admittedly, it was no great shakes compared to the highlights of Sydney and Melbourne, but the neon sign of a moose upending a cocktail and the noise of the mainly young backpacker crowded bar appealed to her.

The alcoholic hit from the Slippery Nipple cocktail acted like oil upon the waters of her previous turmoil. After her third one, the world was definitely looking much better. The DJ ended his set of 80s cheese and was refreshing his drink, when Sarah decided to head outside for a smoke. She barely had time to pull out her pack of Marlboro Reds and put one in her mouth when a lighter appeared, as if from nowhere, and a finger clicked the flame on.

Instinctively, she leant forward and lit the cigarette from the flame. The latter-day Prometheus was a small girl, somewhere in her mid-twenties, Sarah guessed, with cropped black hair.

"Different end of the planet, still clean air fascists, eh?" she said to Sarah, accompanying it with a wry smile. The accent was Midlands English.

"Too right," said Sarah, the cigarette still clamped between her teeth. The two girls smoked in silence for another minute, then Sarah, loath to lose another potential friend, said. "Thanks for the light. Can I buy you a drink, err..."

"Alison," the other girl said.

"Check us Brits out; we bring our bloody stiff upper lips with us," said Sarah.

"A drink would be great," Alison replied. Laughing in unison, the two young women went back inside the bar.

# Balmoral Hotel, Chandler, Northern Territory.

James hadn't quite managed to keep his late-night rendezvous with the delectable Dr Sandersen, falling asleep in his clothes instead. He awoke to the sound of the alarm on his mobile phone ringing which he had mercifully remembered to set the night before.

Staggering to the bathroom he switched on the shaving light to survey the damage. "A shit, shower, shave and I'll be right," he said scratching his unshaven chin.

A little later, he was doing his best to shake the creases out of his one good suit, when there was a knock at the door.

Quickly doing up his bathrobe, he reached into his holdall and brought out a .38 snub nose revolver. This particular model was a street model with the serial number filed off and a heavier hand grip added allowing it to double up as a cosh, just in case you ran out of ammunition. The gun had been James' weapon when he was out on the street in deep cover. Holding the gun down the side of his leg, James stood side on to the door, making himself as small a target as possible.

"Who is it?" he asked quietly. Speaking quietly was a good way of discerning just whereabouts the person outside was standing. If they didn't hear you, there might be a good chance it was two fellows with shotguns waiting to give you the good news.

"Dr Sandersen, bearing aspirin for the afflicted," an urbane voice said, through the door.

"Good enough. Enter," he said opening the door but keeping towards one side.

Impeccably dressed as the night before, but obviously a different outfit, she entered the room, wrinkling her nose as she did. "Y' bunk up with a wombat? I hear they're very prone to do that out here in Bourke," she said.

"I'd save that kind of talk for the Law Society Bar if I were you," said James taking a final look behind her to check the coast was clear, before easing the door closed. "Casting aspersions on the locals won't win you any brownie points round here."

"Scared of the clever Sheila from the big smoke, are they?" she volunteered, casually tossing a packet of aspirin to James.

"Nah, they just prefer to screw possums, that's all."

"Care to join me for breakfast? You look like you could do with a caffeine fix."

"Sure," he said, transferring two aspirins from hand to mouth and following them with a large gulp of water.

"Somebody's thirsty?" she said, nodding to the pile of empty stubbies.

"Got a throat like a badger's arse, if you'll pardon my French," replied James. "But I'd be glad to join you in five."

"You can leave the peashooter here, though," she remarked, nodding to the revolver on the bedside table.

"No can do, I'm, afraid," he said. "I'm a marked man, you know. Eating breakfast could be a risky business," he added. "Do you really want to be machine-gunned over your muesli?"

"Cheap but good, it's a risk I'll take I suppose," she replied, a smile playing across her face as she looked back at James. Cracks were beginning to appear in the good doctor's façade and from where James stood, the light was pouring through.

# Chandler Police Station, Northern Territory.

The briefing room at Chandler Police Station was filled with an assortment of police officers, civilian staff and a non-uniformed element of which James and Sandersen formed a part. Much like the first day of school everyone had formed into their respective groups. James had thought he was being paranoid for a while as he kept imagining that some of the uniform cops were shooting surreptitious glances at him. His fears were soon allayed when he realised their looks were for his sweet-smelling colleague, Dr Sandersen. The pair had made their way to a table via a buffet set out for that morning's briefings.

The room was dominated by a huge map of the Northern Territory on one side and a projector screen and lectern on the other. A group of senior officers milled around the Commissioner, fiddling with files and making last-minute changes to the briefing notes.

Sandersen poured another cup of coffee for James who nodded gratefully and picked up the mug, blew the steam off and took a sip.

"Bloody good this," said James.

"It's all part of the health drive," said Sandersen, acknowledging the Commissioner who was standing in front of a projector screen and having a clip-on radio mike attached to his jacket lapel by another police officer.

"What's that, then?" said James, breaking off part of a croissant and dunking it into his coffee.

"Well he's the architect of the 'Healthy Bodies, Healthy Minds' campaign. His ethos is that cops should be fit and healthy; not tubs of butter who sit in cars all day. So it's out with fry-ups and teas and in with the Fairtrade coffee and granola."

"Gets my vote," said James. "Organic from Papua New Guinea. Will have to take some back to Melbourne with me," he said, tapping the packet of coffee beans.

"Think that'll be any time soon?" asked Sandersen, wistfully.

"Not sure, this one's a real pro, isn't he? Apart from the DNA we've got nothing to go on. He's got half a million square miles of spinifex and dirt to hide in," said James, waving a hand towards the map of the Northern Territory which dominated the far wall.

"Sure, but he's got to eat, got to have a vehicle, got to sleep somewhere. It's not like a city where he can slip back into anonymity. He's either mobile or he's got a hideout and somebody's got to have seen him come and go," said Sandersen.

"So you're saying he's a local boy, then?"

"Well, it's a possibility that's worth entertaining," retorted Sandersen.

"Kirsty Jessop was murdered somewhere other than where she was found; there were fibres of a so far untraceable carpet or rug under her fingernails," said James.

"Which means what, exactly?"

"It means that they're being held for a while and then killed somewhere other than the site where they're being dumped," said James. "But he's also leaving them at places that he knows they'll be found; well, eventually."

"If Constable Campbell hadn't gone back to the Patterson place, she might never have been found," said Sandersen.

"Not likely. This guy's like a cat: he wants to show us his kills," replied James.

The hum of talking people dropped to a murmur as the assembled officers craned to hear the news which being whispered to the Commissioner. Keen to quickly dispel any rumours he strode to the lectern.

"Ladies and gentleman, I have just been informed a body has been found by a stockman just north of the Adelaide

River Roadhouse. Will all members of the 'Nemesis' task force please assemble in the rear car park in fifteen minutes? I'll reconvene this briefing at 3pm this afternoon. Thank you."

With that he snapped off the microphone, and left the briefing room.

Just over twenty minutes later, a convoy of vehicles, three unmarked cars and a minibus drove out of the rear car park of Chandler Police Station. While time was of the essence to catch the killer, for the body sprawled dead in the red dust, the boys in blue would be much, much too late.

# Nr Adelaide River Roadhouse, Northern Territory.

The convoy of unmarked vehicles had been stopped by a uniformed officer several hundred yards from the crime scene. All those aboard had been made to don forensic suits and overshoes before being allowed to cross the tape which cordoned off the scene.

In the years after the case of the murder of British man Peter Falconio and the abduction of his girlfriend, Joanne Lees, the importance of maintaining the integrity of the crime scene for forensic examination had been drilled into every officer.

"Who found her, then?" asked James, his forensic overshoes scuffing up small clouds of dust as he walked towards the tent.

"A stockman by the name of Scott Gillanders," said Collins, opening the flap of the tent to allow James and Sanderson inside. "He was out checking the fences when he saw a gaggle of black kites making a meal out of something," he said, adjusting his hat. "He thought it was one of the water buffalo that had snuffed it, but realised that it was too small."

All three were now inside the tent where a fan ran more to blow away the sickly sweet stench than cool the air.

"Have we got an ID for her?" asked James.

"Yep, Sarah Knight. Twenty-one years old. A Brit on a gap year."

The three looked around the tent, each wrapped in their own private thoughts. After a few minutes, James turned and went outside, pushing the flap as he went. As he stepped under the tape of the inner cordon, a voice stopped him in his tracks.

"Mind if I join you?" said Sandersen, brandishing a packet of Marlboro Reds.

"Sure, why not," he said holding the tape for Sandersen.

The pair made it to the outer cordon where they got out of their forensic suits and overshoes. Sandersen put two cigarettes in her mouth and lit both with a battered Ronson wind-proof lighter, before passing one to James.

"Not dressed for a walk in the bush, was she?" said James exhaling smoke from his nostrils. "I'm guessing she was abducted, killed and then dumped here. What are your thoughts?"

She took a drag on her cigarette and looked across the two-lane blacktop to where uniformed officers were combing the verge in a fingertip search.

"I think she was somewhere comfortable when she was killed."

"Comfortable? What do you mean?," asked James, stubbing the butt of his cigarette out on the post-and-rail fence which separated them from the road's edge.

"She hadn't got any shoes on and she's only wearing a t-shirt. She was probably sitting cross-legged when the killer grabbed her from behind and strangled her," said Sandersen.

"So she didn't get abducted against her will?" asked James.

"Exactly."

"Which means what?" said James, his eyes flitting on the pack of cigarettes in Sandersen's hand.

"Well it means our killer has changed his MO. All the previous victims' bodies showed bruising where they had been dragged against their will. In Stephanie Flanders's case they found one of her flip-flops on the side of the road. Two others had rope marks on their wrists," said Sandersen, proffering the cigarette packet and easing the lid open.

"Surely women are harder to abduct these days," said James, taking a drag on his second cigarette. "Although he's older now, so maybe they're more easily taken in; a sort of friendly uncle appearance?"

"Could be, but I think there's something else, I just can't put my finger on it."

James took a pull on his cigarette and looked on wistfully as a black vehicle bearing the legend "Private Ambulance" arrived to take Sarah Knight's body. Another vehicle had borne her body here and that vehicle was the crux of the investigation as far as James was concerned. He and Sandersen were going to make this their first line of investigation.

# Chandler Police Station, Northern Territory.

"Well it's not like we're trying to avoid catching him, sir," said the Northern Territory Police Commissioner, shifting uneasily in his seat and holding the telephone handset in place with his chin while flicking through a folder crammed with loose printouts.

"Yes, I am aware that the tourists are getting jittery, but flooding the highway with roadblocks has little chance of catching the perpetrator and just builds on the hysteria, sir." A bead of perspiration slid down the back of Caulfield's neck. He had been speaking to the NT Police Minister for a quarter of an hour. Or more correctly, the Minister had been talking *at* him. The upshot of which was "Catch the guy, catch him now!"

"The media, sir? The media side's being run from Darwin… Yes. I've got two full-time staff feeding the mushrooms there," he added. "Brit journos? No not as yet, but it'll soon change. Sarah Knight is English and now we've got another dead, attractive middle-class girl cooling in the morgue. The British tabloid rags will have a field day with it," he added wiping his brow on a Toohey's bar towel. The voice on the other end of the phone concurred with Caulfield on this.

"For sure, they'll run with this 'Highway of Death' crap. It'll be the Falconio case all over again. We'll get portrayed as a bunch of possum-shaggers who couldn't find our dick with two hands and a map."

\*\*\*

Breakfast had once again been splendid, especially for James, who thought back to the lukewarm coffee and stale croissants at the old Armed Offender's Squad. Never having been anointed into the inner sanctum, he hadn't been invited to the brunches at the Temple of Convenience. Then again he wasn't doing five to ten years for corruption and perjury. It was these thoughts that preoccupied him as he peeled himself an orange.

"Penny for them?" Sandersen asked, sidling across to James and putting her coffee cup and saucer down.

"Just thinking that this breakfast is pretty good. Compared to some of my old 'colleagues' who are in choky," he added.

"Glad you didn't take the brown envelope, then?"

"Suppose so," he replied, nonchalantly.

A ripple ran through the room as heads turned towards the lectern. "Officer on deck," a wag shouted. But the remark elicited no response from the Commissioner. He strode to the lectern, shuffled his papers and cleared his throat.

"Ladies and gentleman, your attention, please. I am going to spend a few minutes outlining the autopsy results of our killer's latest victim, Sarah Knight. Once this is concluded we'll review the latest intelligence and then Dr Sandersen will brief us on the psychological profile of the killer we're hunting."

"Finally, your fifteen minutes of fame," said James playfully to Sandersen.

The next fifteen minutes were taken up with the general details of Sarah Knight's post-mortem. Most of this confirmed what James and Sandersen already knew. Sarah Knight had been twenty-one years old, Caucasian and in good health up until the moment a right-handed individual with some strength had grabbed her from behind and strangled her with both hands until she died from asphyxiation, crushing her windpipe in the process. She had drunk alcohol and smoked cannabis in the hours immediately preceding her death and had had unprotected sex with two males, although this was pre-mortem and was probably consensual.

After concluding that, as of yet, no coherent picture had been established of the killer and that all lines of enquiry remained open, the Commissioner left the lectern and took a seat.

Sandersen took up position and without notes began to speak.

"Good morning, ladies and gentlemen. As you will know, I have been asked to form part of this task force and I am hoping to build a psychological profile of our killer. I will now address some of the key points we have concluded so far and then take contributions from the floor."

Over the next hour she outlined the profile she had built of the killer. It was classic textbook stuff from Psychology 101: the lone male, possibly having difficulties forming relationships, etc.

James groaned inwardly and pushed his feet out under the table. He had heard it all before and didn't have the inclination to hear it again. He made a display of pushing back his chair yawning and making his way out of the room. Fishing out a packet of Lucky Strikes he had stashed in his bag, he strode out to the car park. He ran a fingernail across the silver foil, slit it and pulled out a cigarette.

"Still one of the naughty boys at school, eh, James?" said Sandersen with a scowl.

"Who's rattled your cage?" said James not appreciating the intrusion or her demeanour.

"You did, with your yawning antics," she responded, her arms folded and head cocked on one side.

"Well, I wasn't gonna sit there and listen to any more of that schoolboy stuff," said James, disparagingly.

"Well, thanks for your support. It's difficult enough standing up in front of forty blokes without the only out-of-towner skipping out on me," she said.

"So it's them and us, then, is it?" he asked, taking a last drag on his cigarette.

"No, but your support would be appreciated."

"Sure, but that waffle was schoolboy stuff."

"What do you mean?"

"Well, all the studies you quote in your references are from the US and they're based on studies on males in conurbations. Take a look around you, this *is* the urban centre! You're nothing but a bloody tourist here. Throw your guidebook away and get your eyes open."

Without further ado, he stomped out of the car park. A minute later, Dan Collins, dressed in civilian clothes loped after him.

Sandersen was just composing herself, not quite tearful, but a little put out. Begrudgingly at first, she had begun to like James and hoped that their roles as the out-of-towners would build their affinity with each other, but this had been blown away in a glance.

James' anger lasted as far as the other side of the car park. He wasn't even sure why he'd sounded off. He was sorely tempted to go back and put things straight with Sandersen, but before he had a chance he saw Collins strolling towards him.

"Evening, fella," he said.

"Well if it's not my favourite shadow," said James.

"Good to see you too, blue," Collins replied. "Your favourite shadow's just been making sure your urbane arse stays safe out here in big boys' town. You had a visitor but we caught up with him, before he caught up with you. Old geezer, not exactly what you'd expect from a hit-man," said Collins.

"Lead the way, Sancho Panza," said James.

***

Who do you think you are? It's the name for a TV series where celebrity assholes go mooching back into their past to make themselves look like they're ordinary, just like you and me. But they're not, are they? They're just tourists taking a peek into the possible darkness before sailing back into the light. Like the past is like a toy, something we can visit, take out of the proverbial cupboard, play with and then put safely away again. What if you never had any fucking toys? What if the proverbial cupboard is so full of fucking skeletons, there's no room for them? No, that's right, you never had a cupboard, did you, they come in homes, with families. You had a footlocker, the smell of shoe polish and laundry... Church 10.30 mass, the highlight of the week... Father O'Connor, the sickly sweet smell of hair pomade and... a hand sliding down to grab your cock.

Skeletons aplenty... You've never seen their skeletons; the ones from earlier must be bones by now. Never your style that... Leave them intact... let them know what they're missing... going to be missing... A gap year... a fucking gap year...? All laid out for them like a highway, some beer and sunshine before it's back to Blighty, to the mortgage and kids, the husband, a Golf in the drive and the rest of the usual shit...

Just after the dirty deed... when they're cooling... suspended animation... it's good night Vienna, but the heat's still there, peculiar how it lingers...

# Chandler Police Station, Northern Territory.

"What have we got here, then?" said James, flicking open the spy-hole in the door to the cell.

"One Adrian Marsh, former crime reporter and general factotum of *The Darwin Telegraph*. He got the chop from a big daily back in the eighties, left the big city and washed up here about twenty years ago. He's pretty quick off the mark, he likes a drink, but he's no dipso, if you know what I mean," said Collins as he fumbled with a set of keys.

"Okay, let me at him," said James.

The door swung open to reveal a thick-set man in his mid to late fifties, a wonky nose revealing past glories on the rugby field. Rising to his feet Marsh ambled towards James who got an impression of muscle fighting with fat, with neither prepared to give way just yet.

"Adrian Marsh, at your service," said Marsh.

"Ah, Mr Marsh, a pleasure to meet you. I fear my protector here may have been a little overzealous in detaining you as a possible assassin."

Marsh smiled and unrolled his jacket which he had been using as a pillow.

"Can I have my belt and shoelaces back, please, Constable?" said Marsh to Collins.

Grinning sheepishly Collins handed Marsh a box containing his shoes and belt.

"Sorry for the misunderstanding, Mr Marsh," said Collins.

Marsh took out a well-polished pair of brogues and laced them up.

"No worries, Constable, I know that you have orders from on high to keep Mr James safe from the ne'er-do-wells from Melbourne," said Marsh, threading his belt through the loops in his trousers.

"You know me?" asked James trying to conceal his surprise.

"Yes indeed, Commissioner Caulfield told me that you were here. We're old drinking buddies, from back in the day when I was a crime reporter at *The Age*. Back in the days when I still caught a tram to work."

"A cop and a journo seem like an unlikely pairing?" said James, trying to regain his composure.

"It would nowadays, but back then there were no press officers and everyone did business in the pub," said Marsh. "Talking of pubs, why don't we celebrate my new-found freedom with a drink and I can impart my wisdom to you."

"Sounds like a champion idea," replied James, warming to Marsh.

Even amidst the sterile surroundings of an outback police station, Marsh with his brogues and distinct turn of phrase exuded urbanity, something which James had missed amongst the more straight-talking cops like Collins and Toohey.

James followed Marsh to a beaten-up Mitsubishi saloon and the pair got in.

"I'm normally a guy for the pub, but as gossip spreads round here like the clap through a regiment in a whorehouse, I suggest we return to *chez* Marsh and crack a bottle of my finest malt. Then we can see how we can catch this crazy guy who's killing all these pretty women. Can't let him keep doing that: if the pretty tourist girls stop coming to town, then I'll really do my fruit," said Marsh as he gunned the engine and headed out of town.

"What makes you think it's a *he* exclusively?" posed James, one hand splayed on the dashboard and another holding on dearly to the strap near his head.

"Well, nine times out of ten it usually is. Plus, why would a woman murder pretty girls?" added Marsh, peering ahead as a road train hove into view along the two-lane blacktop.

"That's a safe bet." James issued a silent prayer to no god in particular as Marsh accelerated and passed the road train at top speed. They made it.

"So much for the big city cop," said Marsh in a mocking tone. James snapped his eyes open in embarrassment.

"Was that your first time?" asked Marsh.

"First what?" asked James.

"Road train... or the steel dragons as we call them – we all love freaking you city types by burning them off," said Marsh, shooting James a sideways glance.

"Well it bloody worked," said James, shifting in his seat.

"This is us," said Marsh, taking a left off the blacktop and onto a track which he seemed to have chosen at random. The car raised a plume of red dust as the car nosed through the gap in the spinifex and scrub that made up Marsh's drive.

"Just over the next ridge," Marsh said swerving to avoid the desiccated corpse of a kangaroo.

A few moments later a scatter of buildings appeared.

"Home, sweet home," said Marsh, slowing the car down and making for the centre of the huddle of buildings. "Five hundred acres, some buffalo, the dog and me," he said spreading his arms wide.

"How did an inky fingers like you end up with this?" James asked.

"A great uncle left it to me about twenty years ago. There I was doing the court circuit, up to my neck in gangsters and their gory antics. Suddenly I get a call from a firm of lawyers telling me I've got a dingo reservation to come and claim. Quite a day in all," said Marsh.

The men got out of the car and Marsh led the way to a two-storey mock-colonial style house and opened the front door, which appeared to have been left unlocked. James followed the veteran hack into his lair. The front door opened onto a large open space with a staircase taking up one side and two doors to the right, one of which was slightly ajar.

"Time for that whisky, methinks," said a disjointed voice from behind the door. There was some clunking and then the sound of a filing cabinet opening. "Well come in, dear boy," the voice said.

James pushed the door open and went through. Marsh was unscrewing the cap off a bottle of Isle of Jura scotch. He was seated by a desk which seemed to James to be the size of a small battleship. It was covered entirely in piles of loose papers and folders bound with elastic bands, save for an up-to-date PC and a desk lamp with a green glass shade.

"Take a seat over there," said Marsh, gesturing to a leather club chair. He swung round to the table that was adjacent to the window in his chair and filled two tumblers with ice and swinging around again, liberally sloshed scotch into them and pushed one towards James.

"Slainte," said James.

Marsh replied in return and the two men chinked their glasses together briefly.

"So tell me all you know about The Dingo," said James.

\*\*\*

A dark rainy afternoon in the English Midlands; school's out and you're getting off the bus. There's a light drizzle over the town and the sodium orange of the street lights is casting passers-by in a strange hue. Not that they were giving you much attention as they huddle into their coats or take shelter under umbrellas and hurry by. The wind whips around your legs, the thin school tights offering you little protection from the bitter cold. Your fellow pupils scuttle off in groups, eager to get back to their homework if they're conscientious, their games consoles if they're not.

You usually do yours in the comparative warmth and safety of the library, by half past three to four o'clock most of the dossers and lechers have gone home or sought refuge in the plethora of the pubs which dot the town. But homework is pretty far from your mind this dark afternoon. The Tudors, burning Catholic bishops and the annual GDP of Burkina Faso are not top of your agenda.

For three Fridays on the trot he's been waiting for you, on the corner. Waiting patiently, not so much like a wily predator, but more like an expectant dog waiting for its owner. Nonetheless, it still freaks you out. He knows your route, knows you want to just get to the library. Not that he's done anything untoward to you, just come towards you and said that he knows you and has something very important to tell you. But you've heard the stories about these nonces, they've always got a good line in chat, a mental hook, then a ride in the car, then the dog walker, the rich, tangy smell and the lines of policemen in white plastic suits, like the little girl dumped near that village.

No, not going to be you. You grip the Swiss Army knife tightly in your hand inside the pocket of your Parka. "Shit!" You know worse words than that but it'll do... he's there. Average height, average weight, well-dressed and not in the least bit creepy looking. He's coming towards you.

"Alison, Alison! Just wait a minute." He's got a strange accent, certainly isn't local. You quicken your pace, so does he, you look to cross the street but the traffic's too thick and fast...

He's close enough you can smell his breath, coffee and mints. "Please, Alison, just give me a minute, it's important," he says, leaning towards you. Close, too close.

You go for the knife, biggest blade already out. "Piss off, you perv," you scream lunging wildly at him.

He jumps back, surprisingly quickly for someone of his age, you think. He takes a few steps back, both his hands raised up in front of him, palms out defensively.

You keep the knife raised at arm's length. You both face each other, both breathing heavily, eyeing each other up, not unlike the gladiators from Roman times you studied in history.

"Look, I'm not a perv, I don't want to hurt you. I just want to talk to you," His voice is wavering and his eyes are watery like he's holding back tears. Is he genuine? "I've got something I want you to read. It's inside my coat, I'm going to reach it out and put it down here, then I'm going to walk away and when I've gone please pick it up. Is that okay?" His voice and eyes pleading.

"Okay," you say, "but then you better fuck right off," you say, trying to sound tough, and back up your words with action, lunging with the knife at him.

Taking the hint he backs up a few paces, his hands still raised up, palms outwards, and then he slowly drops his left hand into the pocket of his coat. It's a white envelope with the flap taped up and "Alison" in neat handwriting written across the front, nothing else. You'll dwell on this more later, but for now you keep your eyes fixed intently on him, to make sure he's not using the letter as a chance to get you with your guard down. But he's genuine. He leans the envelope against the brickwork of a shop and backs away, then turns on his heels without another look or sound.

Later that night, homework done, face washed, teeth brushed, prayers said, you firmly close the door to your bedroom, listen to make sure they're busy downstairs. It's Wogan talking to some film star, you hear them both sharing a laugh: the coast is clear.

You take the envelope from where you've hidden it amongst the pages of your geography textbook and put it on your desk, turning on the lamp, and turn the envelope over in your hands a few times. No address or other distinguishing mark. It's taped shut with two strips of Sellotape. You fish out the knife from your desk drawer, remembering the look on his face as you lunged for him. You ease the blade through the tape and open the envelope. Single sheets of watermarked "Basildon Bond" or "posh paper" as you know it, used for writing to aunties to thank them for Christmas presents. The same neat handwriting.

You read and reread the letter four maybe five times, your head hurting as a torrent of emotions hit. You feel hot and cold all at once, tears well in your eyes and you feel like throwing up. You put the letter back in the envelope, put it back in its hiding place and get under the covers... You hold the knife for a feeling of safety, large blade out. If Martin comes in to "tuck you in", you'll stick it right in him and twist it.

# Marsh Ranch, Northern Territory.

John Coltrane's *Blue Train* bellowed out loudly and a cloud of cigar smoke blew through the house. Marsh and James were half way down the bottle of Jura and well down a couple of Romeo Y Julieta Cuban cigars with which Marsh's humidor was liberally supplied.

Marsh sat amidst a swathe of paper, photocopied documents, yellowing police reports and bound folders of newspaper cuttings. James had, as an off-the-cuff remark, asked to see what Marsh had put together on The Dingo Case, something which he now minorly regretted, as Marsh opened the third lidded box of documents. Between the plumes of smoke and horn solos, Marsh had outlined some of the key facts and his observations of the original murders. Like all journalists, Marsh loved a conspiracy theory, and his version of events spelt "cover-up" in sky-high letters.

"So they were having a hard time finding anyone for the frame and Calvin Miller fell into their story like a gift from above," said Marsh, sending a plume of smoke ceiling-bound. "Aged twenty-eight, dishonourably discharged from the army, a string of convictions and no alibis. Perfect for the classic fit-up," he added.

"Except he wouldn't exactly play ball, would he?" asked James, swilling his scotch round in his glass.

"Nope, they arrested him, questioned him, bailed him and let him go."

"But he got wind of the fit-up from an anonymous source in the media," said James.

"Exactly," said Marsh with a knowing look.

"So he decided to make for Darwin for a ship to Java, and gets stopped by a lone officer outside Daly Waters," said James.

"Except the officer was a tub of lard who should have retired years before and Miller was ex-army and built like a tank. So Miller slotted the cop, stole his gun and car and legged it," said Marsh.

"Until he ran out of juice just short of Katherine," said James tapping the spot on Marsh's scale map of the Northern Territory.

"Ah, the best laid plans of mice and men," said Marsh. "So he takes off on foot until the net closes around him and he holes up in a deserted farmhouse. He gets surrounded and the shooting starts. Being handy with a gun, he kills two uniforms and wings two others." He picked up the scotch and flourished it at James, who held up his tumbler for a refill. "So, keen not to lose any more officers they fire in some tear gas to flush him out. But instead of flushing him out it sets the house ablaze and Mr Miller has to be identified from his dental records."

"And for years, everyone's happy to let the blame for the killings lie firmly at Miller's door. Until bodies of young girls start turning up again, which is how we got here," said James.

"And so endeth today's lesson," said Marsh, staggering unsteadily to his feet. "I gotta take a piss, Officer, and then I am away to my bed. The spare room's through there," he said, jabbing an arm in the direction of the corridor.

Marsh's bedroom door slammed to. He clattered around for a few minutes, then silence, followed a few minutes later by ragged snoring. James stretched out on the sofa, swirling the shrunken remnants of the ice rocks in his glass of scotch. He felt a sudden surge of energy and rush of insight, admittedly brought on by the scotch, but it also went beyond this – a sort of mental second wind. He realised that spending all his time in the incident room and hotel had clouded his thinking and that despite the booze and music he was feeling a sense of perspective that he hadn't felt for a while. Leaving off the co-codamol had helped and even though his arm hurt more, the trade-off was worth it.

While Marsh had been loquacious and slightly rowdy during the evening, James knew that the journalist had not merely stumbled upon these files. They were the result of months, no, years of work done in his free time. *Here,* James thought, *lay the answer to the case.*

Forget profiling and DNA. Sure, they played their part, but cases had been solved since the dawn of time without them. Sometimes it just came down to plain old-fashioned police work, following the lines of enquiry, collating the evidence and joining the dots up to make the final picture. An investigation was an equation of factors: get these right and you had your man. James took up a pad of lined paper that lay on a side table, took up a felt tip and began doodling, making a rough spider diagram with labels such as "suspects", "motives", "victims".

After an hour he had built a comprehensive picture of the case. Something was building; a nugget of information had lodged in his investigative conscience. "Fuck," he said out loud to no one but himself. He realised that he loved this job more than anything else in his world. Did people who sold software get the same elation? He thought not, but then again he didn't give a shit either way. Out there was someone hellbent on killing. Killing young women, women who were on the cusp of a long and fulfilling life, career, marriage, kids or maybe not. Maybe they'd end up cooling on a piss-stained mattress with a load of bad gear in their arm, but either way they had the right to live a life whatever and not have it snatched away. So what was the cost/benefit for the killer? What did he gain from their loss? "Therein lies the rub?" said James to himself with a wry chuckle.

He hadn't felt this surge of elation since... Since Quantico. Those 385 wooded acres on a Marine Corps base in Quantico, Virginia about thirty-six miles outside Washington, DC.

James had spent eight weeks on secondment from the Metropolitan Police to undergo an "Enhanced Criminal Detection and Mapping" course. A shared room in a dorm, early morning runs through the foggy Virginia Woods, a canteen breakfast. Lectures and an early night after a gathering in the alcohol free "bar" – nips from a bottle of smuggled in booze, the lithe young woman, Katya, twenty-seven, on secondment from the Russian FSB... James drifted into sleep.

He awoke with a raging thirst and a raging hard-on. He'd been dreaming of Sandersen when his leg fell off the sofa and he was pulled back into the early dawn light of another Territory day.

He pushed off the blanket he'd been sleeping under and went through to the kitchen to get some water. After slaking his thirst he sat back down in the living room. He was rearranging the chart he'd drawn the previous evening into some sort of order when his eye caught upon a framed photograph. . It showed a pretty young woman in her twenties wearing a business suit and smiling out of the picture.

"Beautiful, isn't she?" said Marsh. He stood a few feet behind James.

"Sorry, I didn't mean to pry," he said, detecting a sense of tension from Marsh.

"No worries, it's my daughter, Jane, on her twenty-first. She died from leukaemia three years ago. It was a real shock. Her mum Pauline got hit by a lousy drunk driver ten years ago. The only consolation is that she wasn't around to see Jane go the way she did. That's why I'm here on my lonesome," said Marsh, sighing deeply and putting the picture back gently on the desk.

"Hard lines, mate. She's really beautiful," said James, keen to move off the maudlin subject. Marsh detected the mood.

"I know what it's like to lose a kid through no fault of your own. That's why I want to help you catch this bastard," said Marsh.

"Coffee, that's what I need," said James, stretching out and making for the kitchen.

"I'll get the frying pan out and see if we can grease our wheels," Marsh said.

"Sounds like a plan," said James and disappeared from the kitchen. Marsh busied himself finding ingredients for a fry-up from the fridge and cupboards. Suddenly James' head reappeared through the door.

"I know I'm supposed to be a detective, but where's the shower?" The two men laughed.

"Straight up the stairs, left and through the office. It gets everyone who stays here," said Marsh.

James padded up the stairs, took off his clothes, wrapped a towel around him and got under the shower. The force of the water nearly knocked him off balance; Marsh's shower was something else compared to the dribbly lukewarm shower at the hotel, which James thought of as more akin to someone holding a watering-can above his head. The hot water sluiced over him and began to drive out the woolly-headedness the booze from the previous evening had caused him to feel. It was what James called a footprint hangover, not a full rattling skull one, with monster breath and the thick tongue, but nonetheless, a reminder that you really should have taken it easier.

After a good ten-minute shower, James stepped out of the bathroom. He had pretty much soaked the bath towel Marsh had given him. He went into the airing cupboard at the top of the stairs and began sifting through the layers of clothes and sheets for a towel. He moved a layer of folded shirts and uncovered a porno magazine. "Every man's got needs to fulfil, I suppose," said James to himself before replacing the shirts and closing the door. He went back to the bathroom, towelled his hair and was putting toothpaste on his toothbrush when the penny dropped. "Fuck me!" he shouted and ran downstairs to find Marsh.

***

"So run it by me one more time," said Marsh, mopping up tomato juice from his plate with some toast. James put his coffee down and wiped the back of his hand across his mouth.

"Well it's like this. What's been baffling me, the intangible thing I couldn't grasp was why he's been murdering them. I mean what's the motive?"

"Well that's what can't be established, isn't it?" queried Marsh.

"Yes, but all the headshrinkers like Sandersen have even missed this," said James.

"Missed what?" said Marsh.

"The lack of sexual motive. You won't have read the case notes but there's not been any incidence of rape or sexual interference. No one's raised this yet, but it's got to be important. Look at the facts. He's kidnapping attractive young women and not touching them? There's got to be something peculiar about that. Now I'm not a shrink but it's an avenue we've at least got to explore," said James.

"Sure thing, I think you need to get back to town and put this theory to your pretty shrink colleague, Dr Sandersen, and I'll try and get my hands on a statement that managed to lose itself many moons ago," said Marsh.

"Another line of enquiry?" asked James.

"For me to know and you to find out later," said Marsh, tapping his nose.

"Okay, it's a deal. Can you give me a lift back to town?"

A few minutes later they were bowling back along the blacktop with Marsh bawling loudly to Neil Young and James fervently hoping they would not meet nor pass any road trains.

# Balmoral Hotel, Chandler, Northern Territory.

The fax from the Darwin-based forensics lab had arrived as James and Sandersen were once again involved in a rambling argument over the benefits and drawbacks of psychological profiling of killers. The discussion was free-wheeling and good-natured. James was sensing that the previous tension was over and that he and Sandersen were friends again after his outburst. He was further encouraged in his pursuit of the good doctor after the previous night's protracted and tearful phone call to Monica, his girlfriend in Melbourne. The need to hide from the attentions of Bain's henchmen had finally taken its toll and she was leaving James to go back to the UK to live and make a fresh start.

"I'm not going to play the grieving widow, with a folded flag and a framed picture of you to keep me company," she had said to James, as if she had some sort of omnipotent power.

His wounded arm had begun to hurt like a bastard since then and he had once again reached for the co-codamol and had to don the sling, attracting the chagrin of Johnson and the other cops. The sympathy it had elicited from Sandersen had more than compensated for this however.

# Supermax, HM Prison Barwon, Nr Geelong, Victoria.

Cyrus Bain had had a rude awakening. At three-thirty that morning a group of fresh guards had rousted him out of his bunk, cuffed and shackled him and put him in an isolation cell. They had tossed his cell and confiscated the contraband they had found. He had been given some breakfast and told him his lawyer would be with him shortly. Bain knew the drill and had been civil to the guards and compliant when they had cuffed him. He knew how to play the game; this was just a swift clampdown, the enthusiasm for which would rapidly wane. Soon the twin temptations of easy money and the boredom of the job would hit home, and he would re-establish his fiefdom. He was stretched out on the thin mattress contemplating a future strategy when there was rattling on the cell door and the hatch in the door opened.

"Stand up, Bain. You've got to get dressed for your boyfriend," said the guard sardonically.

Bain slid off the bunk and put his hands behind his head in a gesture of compliance. The door opened and two guards marched in. One put his boot on the inside of Bain's foot. The second moved behind him.

"Stretch your arms out and look along towards the wall," snapped the second guard. Bain did as he was told, the cuffs went on and were ratcheted up, not too tight to be painful, but tight enough to mean business. Grabbing an arm apiece the guards frogmarched Bain into a visitor's room. It was bare except for two chairs and a table, all of which were bolted down to the floor and offered little in the way of comfort. The guards pushed Bain into a chair and then left. The door closed; there was no handle on the inside. Still cuffed, Bain made himself as comfortable as possible and began reading a poster on the dangers of drug smuggling.

Bain's "boyfriend" turned out to be a junior lawyer from Appleton Winch, one of Melbourne's most prestigious law firms. The presence of the young man in the badly fitting suit was a snub to Bain and a none-too-subtle reminder that his stock had fallen recently.

"Mr Bain, it's good to meet you at last," said the man.

"Good to meet you, too. So what progress has been made with my lawsuits?" asked Bain. The lawyer shifted in his seat and extracted a sheaf of papers from his briefcase.

"Well Mr Bain, I am happy to tell you that the plaintiff in the first case has been settled. However, the second case is proving more difficult to settle, we are looking to bring the case to an informal end, as soon as possible."

"Excellent," said Bain.

With little said, but much understood, the nervy young legal eagle swept his papers into his briefcase and knocked on the door. A few seconds later the door was opened by one of the guards and Bain was left alone once more. He had just resumed his reading of the drugs poster when the door opened again. The guards stomped in and Bain got to his feet. They took him back to his cell. Bain sat down on the mattress and looked around him. Something dug into his backside.

Bain ran his hand under the thin blanket. It came upon a rolled-up magazine held fast by two elastic bands. He rolled them off and flattened the magazine out, inside was a mobile phone. Bain chuckled to himself and realised now why a nonentity like the guy he'd met had been sent. Bain turned the phone on, tiptoed across to the cell door and listened for any activity. Satisfied the coast was clear, he punched in a number.

# Chandler Police Station, Northern Territory.

"The *grand fromage* calls, I'll be back as soon as," said James looking balefully at Sandersen.

He followed the young woman down the corridor. She knocked on the door and opened it before beating a hasty retreat.

"Good luck," she mouthed as she made off down the corridor.

Caulfield was on the phone, clutching the handset as he paced between his desk and the window. Dark patches showed under his arms despite the air-conditioning being on full blast.

"Yes sir, it's our first priority. Of course, sir," said Caulfield, putting the phone down.

"James, sorry about that, fucking politicians!" he said, slumping in his chair and gesturing for James to take a seat. "It seems we're going to be losing you for a while. Your favourite gangster's trial has been brought forward."

"How come?" asked James.

"It seems that one of his fellow competitors for Melbourne's number one scumbag jumped to his death from the sixth floor of the remand centre. Suffice to say Big Bernie Jenkins won't be costing the state any more money."

James couldn't hold back a chuckle.

"Well good riddance to the bastard, whether he was jumped or whether he was pushed," said Caulfield.

"Last of the old school gangsters," said James. "Trouble is, now Big Bernie's road kill, they'll be looking to fill his shoes, or more likely Bain will."

"Which makes it paramount you get back to Melbourne and get them to throw away the key on him," said Caulfield.

"Indeed, sir," replied James.

"You take a Cessna to Darwin tomorrow and then catch a charter flight. Two of my men will accompany you. Business class none the less," smiled Caulfield. "Safe journey and come back soon."

# Balmoral Hotel, Chandler, Northern Territory.

Lawrence James was taking a sip of his whisky when there was a knock at his door. Placing the whisky on the table he moved his hand across to the .38 revolver and picked it up.

"Come in," he said raising the gun towards the door. Sandersen gingerly eased the door open.

"Take it easy, it's just a soft handed academic from the big city," said Sandersen, with an easy smile.

"Looks like I'm back to Melbourne. The chief's just given me my marching orders."

"Back to the bosom of your own force," said Sandersen with resignation.

"Hardly, I'm *persona non grata* after turning Queen's evidence on that bunch of bastards in Armed Offenders," he sighed.

"But they all got busted, didn't they?" said Sandersen.

"Well, the media got wind of it. There were a few light jail sentences, you know, token charges of assault. But a lot of the higher-ups got away. Even the guys that did time still got a slice of the kickback fund."

"For taking the fall?" asked Sandersen.

"Precisely," he said with a downcast look and swallowed the last of the whisky.

"Sometimes you've got to take a stand and live with the consequences," said Sandersen.

"True, but it doesn't half piss you off when one of your ex-colleagues sticks his finger up at you as he roars off in his Merc while you're sitting at the traffic lights in your junk pile."

"Point taken."

"We can't all write best-selling books on cod psychology either," said James with a smirk.

"Why, you shit!" said Sandersen making a half-hearted attempt to slap him.

James caught her hand and pulled her closer. She fell towards him and when he caught her in his arms and made to kiss her she didn't flinch. They collapsed onto the bed and began tearing at each other's clothes.

# Fairmile Airfield, Northern Territory.

The Fairmile Airfield was a rejuvenated World War Two RAAF Station. A single runway and a cluster of beaten-up looking Nissen huts played host to a small number of fixed-wing planes and a couple of helicopters. Some were the playthings of weekend flyers but most were work-horses ferrying staff and supplies to outlying cattle stations. It was also an ideal place for a discreet flight, which was why Caulfield had nominated it as James' point of departure for Melbourne.

James had been picked up at the back entrance to the hotel by Detectives Fenwick and Lampeter earlier that morning. He had nicknamed his protectors Morecambe and Wiser after their physical and habitual resemblance to the wildly popular comedy duo whose Christmas Specials had been the highlight of the James family Christmas TV watching.

Fenwick was the older, taller guy with glasses and a sardonic wit.

Lampeter was smaller, slightly tubby and always ready with a quip. He had been dubbed "Wiser" as he had a masters in criminology from Melbourne University. He had been keen to hear more from James about his time at Quantico and his initial resentment at being pulled off The Dingo investigation was soon tempered by the chance to speak to his new charge. Lampeter was deeply engrossed in conversation with James about the effectiveness of psychological profiling as Fenwick gunned the car through the open gates of the airfield and pulled to a halt.

The airfield apron was deserted save for a sole Piper Cherokee light aircraft that was parked to the side of the airstrip. Next to it was a fuel truck which moved off with a bellow of fumes as the civilian Toyota Land Cruiser slowed to a halt next to the plane.

The fuel truck drove through the gates and off down the road. Fenwick got out and walked towards a pot-bellied man who wore oil stained overalls and was wiping the sweat from his forehead with a dirty neckerchief.

"Morning, mate," the man said. "She's all fired up and ready to go, your bog rats in the shed," he said, gesturing to the portacabin across the tarmac.

"Cheers, mate," said Fenwick.

"No worries," said the man dismounting the steps he had been standing on, picking up his toolbox before disappearing in to the dark interior of a nearby hangar. James and Lampeter had stacked the three men's collective luggage in a pile at the side of the plane.

"D' y' like flying?" asked Lampeter, nudging a well-polished shoe against his battered suitcase.

"It's okay with hot and cold running hostesses and an in-flight movie, not so keen on these crates," said James, nodding towards the plane.

"Beats two days on the loser cruiser though, I bet?" said Lampeter.

"Certainly does," agreed James.

Fenwick came out of the nearby portacabin with another man. "This is the guy who's getting us out of here: Stan Curtis, ex-Vietnam fighter ace," said Fenwick, with a wry smile. Curtis was wirily built, had cropped salt and pepper hair and leathery skin from too much sun and too many cigarettes.

"'Nam, really?" said Lampeter.

"Sure thing, no fighters though. I just flew transports from one place to another. No great shakes, really," said Curtis pulling a wrinkled packet of Camels from his pocket and walking off. "Got the time I take to smoke this and get back to stow your luggage and get onboard."

"Sure thing, El Capitano," said James, making the wanker sign behind Curtis's back.

Lampeter sniggered as he picked up his gear and got into the plane. Fenwick followed suit, taking a quick look around before he followed James onto the plane. After a bit of shuffling and stowing, the three men had themselves sat down.

Curtis returned to the plane, slammed the passenger door shut and climbed into the cockpit. He began his pre-flight checks and put on his headset.

"You'll need to get a headset on each or you won't hear a bloody thing," Curtis said. The men did as he said and donned their headsets.

"Close as you'll ever get to being a DJ," quipped Lampeter to Fenwick who flicked him the V-sign in response.

"Ok, here we go, guys. Buckle up," shouted Curtis as he turned the engine over. The three men did up their seatbelts and sat back. The aircraft taxied up the concrete strip and took off smoothly into the air.

Curtis levelled out of a steep climb and settled at just over 15,000 feet. Below, the panorama of the Northern Territory unfolded. A swathe of red earth dotted with spinifex and occasional rocky outcrops spread out below.

James imagined the cool pools, which lay in the lee of the rocky outcrops. Sparkling clear water, but, like with most of Australia, danger lurked all too closely, in the form of freshwater crocodiles.

The thought jogged James' mind back to the time when he had visited the Northern Territory during his gap year nearly fifteen years previously. He'd met Nicola, a fellow Brit, during a hangover breakfast at a down-at-heel café. Romance – or more probably loneliness and lust – had blossomed over the curdled bacon and eggs and they had spent two weeks touring the Top End in a battered Nissan Patrol. Top of James' memories was the alfresco swimming and sex at the pools which were dotted around the territory. For Brits coming from a damp, crowded island, the experience was one to be savoured. He was snapped out of his reverie as Fenwick bumped into his knees on the way to the cockpit.

"Off to sit on the captain's knee?" quipped Lampeter.

"Fuck off, Lamp, just because you're cacking your pants with fear!" snapped Fenwick.

James was too pissed off with Fenwick to bother joining in and merely diverted his eyes across to the adjacent window. Fenwick brushed the curtain aside and went into the cockpit. The other two men took their headsets off and tried to make the most of the limited space they had and closed their eyes in a vain attempt to catch some sleep.

James was giving much thought to taking the lithe Dr Sandersen for a similar trip to the seemingly undiscovered pools around the region. With these serene thoughts he drifted into a blissful doze.

# Stuart Highway, Northern Territory.

Plunger handles are fine for cartoon characters and mobile phone detonators are the mark of a true amateur. But a true professional of the trade likes to use their own little nuances when making a bomb. This was very much the case of Tyler Smith, one of those rare bomb-makers who did not have a military background.

Back in the early nineties, Smith, ever the entrepreneur, had taken advantage of the newly porous Iron Curtain and headed east with a holdall full of US dollars. He left Archangel a few months later with enough plastic explosive to run a full-scale bombing campaign for several years. It was the fag-end of this material that he had used in his latest work for Bain.

Half a kilo, to be precise. A little overzealous maybe, but there was no chance of collateral damage so why not do a thorough job?

And the detonator for this little bundle of joy? His signature device – a mercury tilt switch. With a modern twist – once the device went off a text message would be emitted with the GPS co-ordinates and the chance to review the fruits of his labours.

***

Half an hour's flying time from Fairmile, the little plane was cruising at 15,000 feet altitude with clear skies and no wind. Curtis kept the airspeed on the low side. He was only taking the one trip today and the more fuel he conserved the better. He had plans for an overnight stay and perhaps would even manage a visit to a Darwin massage parlour staffed by delicate and beautiful Vietnamese girls, the kind he'd first got to know in Saigon during the Vietnam War.

"Down there is Donovan's Cross," said Curtis, pointing to a cluster of farm buildings and houses down below.

"A cattle station?" asked Fenwick.

"Yeah, about 10,000 cows. This is where we make a turn for Darwin. You better tell the guys to strap themselves in," said Curtis.

"Sure thing," said Fenwick, giving the thumbs up sign and pushed the curtain aside and stuck his head into the rear cabin.

"Guys we're going to be turning in a sec, so belt up, will you?"

Lampeter tapped James on his shoulder and he got the gist. Fenwick disappeared behind the curtain and back into the cockpit.

"What a pain in the arse!" said Lampeter. "Five minutes up in front and he thinks he's Douglas Bloody Bader!"

"Douglas who?" asked James.

But Lampeter didn't get the chance to answer. The plane banked left and almost instantly the cabin turned into a ball of heat, light and sound. James was blinded and deafened by the intense explosion and lost all sense of his surroundings. He felt the heat dissipate and a rush of cold thin air just before he blacked out.

\*\*\*

The familiar beeping of an incoming text message roused Tyler Smith from his unplanned nap. He had nodded off as he sat in the driver's seat of his Land Rover Discovery. He picked up his mobile phone and clicked on the letter icon. "Package delivered", it read.

He allowed himself a quick smirk of satisfaction, put his phone back in its dashboard holder, pulled down his Aviator sunglasses and started the engine. The air-conditioning kicked in taking away some of the stupefying heat. But modern technology could do nothing to stop the plumes of red dust he made as he gunned the vehicle over the rough terrain, crushing spinifex as he drove. Not that he needed GPS to find his destination. The plume of acrid black smoke rising to the West like a mini Hiroshima provided more than an adequate guide.

Smith reckoned on having approximately ninety minutes to check on his handiwork and make himself scarce before any punter or the forces of law and order made themselves known. Plus, even if they did, he would relish a little action. He was, as the saying goes, loaded for bear with an M16 rifle, a sawn-off shotgun for close up work, a Desert Eagle handgun and a pair of hand grenades purloined from the US military stores at the Pine Creek Base.

Smith decided he would circle the crash site a couple of times, before going in on foot to take a closer look. Bain wanted photographic evidence before any electronic bank transactions were made. *Fair enough, really,* thought Smith as he made a first wide circle of the crash site.

# Brayford River Valley, Northern Territory.

ate is a fickle friend and for Lawrence James the chips had fallen well. When the mercury tilt switch had triggered the half kilo of Semtex, the little plane had been blown into two pieces. The force of the blast had gone forward towards the cockpit, and Curtis and Fenwick had been eviscerated. The tail section of the plane had sheared off and fallen to earth, landing in the deep water of a creek before coming to rest on the right bank. The tail section and a swathe of detritus from the plane fuselage and the contents of the three men's luggage were strewn around. It was this scene that Smith surveyed as he scanned the area from the vantage point of a rocky outcrop above the meandering creak.

"Fistral Beach will be fine, with good breakers and a steady wind of six knots," groaned James as he came round again. He had been lapsing in and out of consciousness for some time. Aware of this, he'd been trying to engage his critical faculties through constant repetition of the phrase. He'd learnt this as a tactic to fight off the onset of hypothermia during an outdoor survival course in the rain-swept Brecon Beacons of Wales. It had also been drilled into him at Quantico as a method of keeping yourself or colleagues conscious after receiving gunshot wounds.

"Fistral Beach will be fine, with good breakers and a steady wind of six knots," James repeated to himself. Surfing had one of the factors for his original move to Australia, James had been a frequent visitor to Fistral, one of the few surfing beaches of note in the UK. It had been a tradition the night before, after packing up the car, to watch the local news and check the weather forecast. The mantra he was repeating was the weather forecast from the best day he'd ever had surfing there.

The desire to sleep ebbed away and a little energy returned to his body. James began to move all parts of his body. He waggled his fingers and toes. "All good so far," he said to himself. Then a burst of pain hit him from his left arm, the one he'd been shot in. A wave of nausea enveloped him and he vomited to the side. *First time for a long time it wasn't the booze that made me barf*, thought James. He was lying in a prone position, his feet just in the edge of the deep creek that flowed sullenly by.

The creek ran through a deep gorge with a narrow belt of trees and bushes forming a ribbon along the edges of the left bank.

"Cover," said James, thanking his lucky stars he'd landed on the left bank. He quickly decided that getting under cover for the immediate future was his best option. Further motivation came from the desire to move away from the recently vacated contents of his stomach. He pulled himself up into a sitting position. His shirt had been blown off and his trousers were tattered rags. Bits of singed hair fell from his scalp. His feet were bare and they, along with most of his body, were covered in a thin film of black soot.

Rolling over into a crawling position, James used his elbows and knees to get to the bank of the creek where he slaked his thirst and tried the best he could to wash off the worst of the soot.

Satisfied, he began the long crawl up the steep bank and into a dense thicket of bushes and trees. Thorns scratched and cut him, causing a profusion of small wounds. James correctly assumed that the adrenaline was insulating him from the worst of the pain for now.

Finally, after what seemed an eternity, he came to rest under a thick bush which had little low growth but a dense upper growth. Here he could lie and survey anyone who came into the gorge and see if they were friend or foe. Happier in this prospect refuge and satisfied with his proximity to fresh water, James decided to spend some time mulling over what had happened and why. Not only would this help him reach a considered decision, it would also take his mind off the throbbing pain in his arm.

First, this was no accident – the explosion came from within the fuselage, ruling out engine failure. So was it a bomb?

If so, who planted it? Probably someone who had access to the aircraft. Curtis had been in the plane and was probably dead, so he was pretty much off the suspect list. These were the thoughts that filled James' mind as he waited for night to fall.

# Fullilove ranch, Brayford River Valley, Northern Territory.

Natalie Vukasin had come to the Northern Territory from her native Poland looking for adventure and instead found love, both of a man and the land he belonged to.

Although a doctorate in political science from Krakow University wasn't the best qualification with which to seek a job as a ranch hand on a cattle outfit, she had, nonetheless, adapted well. She still listened to Chopin at night and could practice the piano in the cool of the evenings with the doors of the ranch-style house thrown open.

Through playing this fellow émigré's music she could remind herself of the flat lands of her country, steeped in blood and history. She had swapped it for this blood-red, austere land but was growing to love it as she learned of the Dream Time from her boyfriend, Clive. An Aboriginal, they had met one day as he wandered across the flat, dusty expanse, where she was mending a fence.

Heavily weighed down with stereotypes, she had apologised profusely when she found Clive spent most of his time working as an IT analyst in Darwin, had a car, an internet connection and that they had a shared love of Chopin.

Misplaced ignorance had quickly turned to keen friendship and their relationship had blossomed. She was thinking of Clive as she drove the pickup down the rutted track towards the creek where she had seen smoke rising.

Her boss, Terry Fullilove, a retired stockbroker from Sydney had radioed her and asked her to check it out. He had seen the plane disappear. Something in the back of her mind had made her sense that this was more than a mere straightforward crash. This feeling caused her to stop the truck and take a rifle from the rack from behind the cab. She pushed in a full magazine and cocked the rifle, before placing the safety catch on and taking a steady amble towards the creek which ran through the rocky gully.

\*\*\*

Tyler Smith was already there. He clutched his M16, the selector switched to three-shot burst. Debris was strewn all around and the soles of his boots were hot from treading over smouldering wreckage. His eye caught a glint of metal. It was Lampeter's watch. His body was camouflaged by a piece of twisted fuselage. Taking no risks, Smith shouldered his weapon and fired a burst into the man's body. It twitched under the impact of the high-velocity rounds.

James was jolted awake by the low thump of the gunshots. Smith's gun had a suppressor fitted to his gun to deaden the noise of the rifle. James knew the report of an M16, from his time at Quantico. He knew it meant trouble, but there was little he could do. He had a raging thirst, was racked with pain and had no weapons. Well, save for his Leatherman tool. In a way of gaining a modicum of reassurance in absence of doing anything more robust, he took it from the pouch on his belt and opened the cutting blade. The heavy metal implement in his hand felt good and gave him a semblance of psychological if not physical security. He crouched lower in his makeshift hideout and closed his eyes in an effort to boost his sense of hearing.

Smith turned the body over with his foot, the stitch-like row of bulletholes across Lampeter's front turned to a mass of bone, blood and devastated internal organs. Lampeter, however, still breathed.

Smith hated cops, but he wasn't a sadist. He raised the gun and fired another burst into Lampeter's head. He didn't look to see if it had done the job. Even Lampeter's own mother wouldn't have recognised him now.

Smith moved off and followed the trail of debris through the gully. He knew the device had probably reduced the rest of them to pulp but he was taking no chances. He saw a briefcase and bent down to look through the contents. Something distracted him from his search. From the other side of the gully came the noise of an approaching vehicle, making hard work of the lunarscape. The gully filtered sounds like a giant funnel and gave Smith more than adequate warning. He snapped the magazine out of his rifle and rammed a fresh one home; dropping into a crouch, he ran to the crest of the gulley.

Rookie cop Howard Chatwin didn't really stand a chance as the ancient Nissan Patrol churned its way up the track towards the gully. He didn't even see the flicker of shadow as Smith hove into view. Preferring effectiveness over finesse this time, Smith opened up on the beleaguered Nissan Patrol on full automatic, emptying the magazine in a matter of seconds. The four-wheel drive's windscreen imploded under the fusillade; bullets had ricocheted off the interior and caused further carnage. Chatwin's torso was a profusion of wounds and his left arm was missing from the elbow down. His chipped wedding band would later be found embedded in the rear of the vehicle. He had died almost instantly.

Gun up and forward, Smith made a circuit of the smouldering and wrecked vehicle. Content that the cop was dead, he reached into his backpack and pulled out an innocuous black box about the size and weight of a full Coke can, which had a flashing diode on it. He pressed a button on a remote control on his belt and the device was armed. He threw it onto the rear seat of the vehicle and made for the ridge. The fifteen-minute delay on the incendiary device would give him time to get clear of the area, before the blaze began. Smith slung his back and loped off, his pistol held low at his side.

\*\*\*

Natalie Vukasin had instinctively hit the deck on hearing the shots. She had been approaching the top of the gully from the opposite direction, crawling with the rifle slightly aloft. She made it to the lip of the gully to see Smith unleash his ambush and the full horror of the aftermath. Her grandpa, who had fought the Germans as a member of the Home Army, had told her of the horrors of the 1944 Warsaw Rising, but she had never yet seen anyone killed.

For some time she had sat numb, possibly a few seconds only, she never really knew. The shock soon turned to anger and she picked up the rifle and looked through the scope, and drew a bead on Smith. His head appeared in the cross-hairs of her sights. She drew breath, realised it and squeezed the trigger. Smith had moved slightly and the shot went wide, blasting a termite mound, causing Smith to drop to the floor. He rolled over, unholstering his gun, and came up in a crouch with his gun forward.

He aimed roughly in the direction from which the shot had come and fired three shots before fleeing.

Vukasin was no firearms expert but knew the shots would pose no risk from that distance. Her chance of hitting a moving target was slim so she turned her attention to Smith's vehicle. In the movies people always shoot out the tyres. In the outback vehicles might run on flat tyres for a few kilometres. She went for the fuel tank, which she had identified was on her side via the fuel filler cap. She fired two shots. There was a delay and the vehicle was engulfed in a spout of flame as the full petrol tank exploded. A cacophony of secondary explosions was set off as Smith's ammunition cooked off. Smith disappeared out of view and Vukasin took a moment to wipe her sweaty forehead and hands.

She changed the rifle's magazine and began to formulate a plan of action. The guy was obviously ruthless; he'd killed a cop and wouldn't think twice about executing her. She needed to get back to her vehicle and get on the radio and raise help. Slinging her rifle she moved off. The sound of an engine caught her attention. Her pickup came up the ridge towards her. She thought it might be the killer. Lacking any cover she dropped to one knee and levelled her rifle ready to fire. Suddenly a head popped out of the driver's window and a pair of hands went up. Guessing the killer wouldn't do this, she stood up and dropped her rifle. The pickup screeched to a halt. The driver got out. He was covered in black dust and dried blood. He brandished something in his hand, said something unintelligible and collapsed in a heap. She picked him up and carried him into the jeep, she got the air-conditioning going and sloshed some water over the prostrate form.

"Lawrence James – Victoria Police," said Vukasin out loud. She held James' torn and burnt warrant card, which bore his picture.

James gave an audible groan and pulled himself upright.

"Shit, what happened?" he said.

"You came to my rescue like a knight of old," she smirked, still high on a mix of adrenaline and terror. "I think you were in the plane that crashed."

"Oh yeah, gotcha," said James.

"Well, should we get going or get after the guy who killed your mates?" she asked.

"We better get going, but you'd better rustle up the cavalry," said James.

"Yes sir, Mister Policeman," said Vukasin, flippantly.

"How do you know I'm a cop?" asked James, looking puzzled.

"Two reasons," she said. "One, the fact everyone wants to see you dead. Two, this," she said, flourishing his torn and burnt warrant card.

"Oh, I see," he said, taking the proffered card.

"Natalie Vukasin at your service."

"Pleased to meet you," said James. "You're not from round here, are you?"

"Nope, Poland," she replied.

"I'm not from around here, either. So we both came here for the scenery, then?" said James.

"Probably. Certainly wasn't for the nightlife," she added.

"You take the rifle – I'll drive," said James.

"Sure thing, comrade," said Vukasin, winking at James.

He turned the ignition and they moved off. He was no military tactician but James knew that cresting the ridge in broad daylight was tantamount to suicide, so skirted the ridge instead.

He couldn't help taking a sneaky sideways glance at Natalie Vukasin. She was in her thirties and clad in the nondescript attire of a ranch hand. Nevertheless, she had a fine bone structure and fine blonde hair dyed by the unforgiving outback sun.

James returned his attention to the front of the truck. At that same instant the windscreen imploded and James was hit in the face by flying glass. Blinded, he jerked the wheel suddenly, causing the truck to swerve wildly. It tipped and rolled down the ridge completely gambolling over twice before coming to rest in a dry creek bed.

*\*\*\**

It's just after 9.30 on a Sunday morning. You told mum, who was ironing in the front room, that you were biking over to Jennie's to do some homework and maybe play on her new computer.

"Fine," she says, over the hiss of the iron. "But remember to be back for your tea," she adds as you go out through the kitchen door to the garage. A thought crosses your mind; you'd better make sure you bike off towards Jennie's – even though it's the opposite way to the train station. You get the bike out of the garage. It's a racer, twenty-one gears, an expensive "gift" from Martin after the first time he'd come to visit you in the night.

Slamming the gate you push off down the hill towards Jennie's house. You double back through the Miner's Welfare Park, pass the smashed-up swings and take a wide circuit around the bandstand whose floor is covered in broken glass, used condoms and cigarette butts. A couple of boys are in there, hunched down, probably rolling a joint. You know it's where Jennie got fingered by two boys last week. She'd said afterwards she would let them go all the way if they bought her a bottle of 20:20 and ciggies. She'd called you frigid and a virgin. Ironic really, cos you'd not been a virgin for over a year. Not since the night Martin had brought a "friend" round to visit you. At least Jennie would be pissed when she lost her virginity. The school nurse had been surprised that you were sexually active. "I hope you're taking precautions?" she'd said.

You brake to a halt. The station car park is empty as you lock your bike up to the railings. The locker key is round your neck on a piece of string. You go in through the doors. You walk to the Coke machine and put in some money, taking the chance to look around. A man behind the glass in the ticket office is reading a copy of the Sun and doesn't look up. An old lady with a huge suitcase is completing the crossword. The can slams down into the tray and you collect it. Satisfied no one is lurking, you go to the lockers. The 200s are mid-way up the bank of lockers. You slot the key in and it opens. You look inside – a dun brown folder and a card with his writing on it.

You slip the card into the inside pocket of your coat and the folder into your school bag, which you'd emptied especially the night before. Where to go? Home? Too risky. The library closed. Somewhere you can read uninterrupted. As you unlock your bike you get an idea. Shakeaway's – tucked down a side street and nearby. You've still got a fiver from this week's family allowance.

A light drizzle is beginning to fall, you pull up the hood of your coat and bike down the High Street, the weight of the bag straining against your shoulders. Shakeaway's banana yellow signboard is out on the street. You brake to a halt, dismount and lock up your bike.

The milkshake bar is empty save for a Goth girl behind the counter and two boys on the table football machine who are engrossed in their game. You order an extra thick raspberry ripple with Cadbury's Flake chunks. The Goth girl says she'll bring it across with your change. You find a corner table facing the window, shake off your coat and take the folder out of the bag. You slide the pile of loose sheets out of it and look at the first one.

You barely notice the Goth girl gently place the milkshake down next to you and slide the coins that make up your change towards you. You appreciate her not attempting to read what you're reading. A few minutes later, you scoop the loose sheets back into your school bag and leave. You need to find a phone box and start living your real life.

\*\*\*

# Brayford River Valley, Northern Territory

Two fixed-wing Pilatus PC-12 aeroplanes had been tasked with finding the crash site of the plane. Doug Fairbanks banked his plane in a westerly direction to make a second sweep of the scorched red earth quadrant he'd been tasked to search.

Smith had heard the sound of the light aircraft just seconds after he had slung his M16 and made off. He wasn't a hundred per cent sure he'd done a total job on the pair, but he knew the cavalry weren't far away. Now he was on foot the game had changed. Luckily, he had stashed some food and water a few miles away in case of such an eventuality. Even though he might not get to collect his pay cheque from Bain, staying alive would have to do for now.

But Smith wasn't as fortunate as he might have thought. A few hundred yards away a man with considerably more bushcraft, and a good measure of cunning and guile thrown in, had him in his sights.

Clive Webb was the name the nuns had given him after he had arrived at the orphanage, having been taken from his parents who he'd never seen again since the man from the Department had come for him and his two sisters.

At fifteen, Clive had simply walked out of the orphanage telling the sisters he was going home. Now aged forty-five, Clive lay prone in a cluster of spinifex as he watched Smith take off at an easy lope, taking a looping route. *Possibly back to the nearest road,* thought Clive. Following him would be too obvious, and he was well armed and wary. *Better to bide my time and take him when the night comes,* thought Clive. The night had been his friend in the past and it would prove a useful ally again soon.

\*\*\*

"Clunk, click, every trip!" said James to Vukasin as they both undid their safety belts and brushed shards of safety glass off their clothing. The pair had come out of the crash relatively unscathed thanks to their forethought – or maybe just from years of instinctively buckling up.

"That plane saved our bacon," said James through a mixture of exhaustion, shock and exhilaration.

"Bacon? Clunk click? What are you babbling about?" asked Vukasin bemusedly.

"Not to worry. Let's get the rifle out of this wreck and then we'll get a signal fire going," said James.

"What are we going to use for that?" asked Vukasin.

"Let me worry about that; you take this and keep doing your sharpshooter act," he said, passing her the rifle and a handful of bullets that he'd scooped out of the footwell.

"Patronising shit!" she replied and took off to the top of the ridge.

James tore off some loose fabric from his already ripped and burnt shirt and set fire to it with his lighter. It caught in the light breeze and he threw it into the interior of the wrecked pickup, which soon caught ablaze. He ran up to join Vukasin who had taken shelter in the lee of the ridge which sought to deflect smoke and flames from the blazing vehicle.

"If the bastards don't see that then we are doomed," said James, in a half-hearted attempt to make amends.

"You've crashed in a plane, crashed in a truck and been shot at, I think you deserve a break, but only this once," smiled Vukasin, wagging a finger in mock concern. James slumped onto the floor next to her. She knelt down next to him. Keen to feel the closeness of a human being she put James' head in her lap and began stroking his tousled hair; In her spare hand she clutched the rifle. Overhead she heard the thrum of a plane's engine. Help was near at hand, or so she hoped.

\*\*\*

Webb finally had his man where he wanted him. He had tracked Smith for several hours through the bush. As Webb had thought, Smith was heading for the road. He'd now stopped and had disappeared into a shallow defile in the ground. No doubt he'd got something stashed there and he'd chosen well, the defile couldn't be seen from any direction until you were upon it.

Smith was crouched in the dell; he scraped with the heel of his boot and dislodged some loose soil and small rocks. The scraping revealed the corner of a dun-coloured tarpaulin, which was almost indistinguishable from the red earth surrounding it.

He rolled the tarpaulin back to reveal a British Army issue Bergen rucksack which was bulging with equipment. He pulled it from its hiding place and set it down. Like a squirrel revealing its concealed horde, he began to remove items from it. Within a few minutes he had strapped on some army webbing and was filling the pouches with essential equipment to make good his escape. This included a Sig Sauer pistol, spare magazines, a combat knife, a water bottle and a map and compass. He would move by night, guided by his most vital piece of equipment, a GPS handset. Now to bury the cache. He unfolded the entrenching tool and got busy.

Webb crossed the two metres in less than a second, but it was enough to alert Smith, who swung the heavy entrenching tool into Webb's leg.

His femur shattered under the impact of the vicious blow, with a sickening crunch. Webb screamed in agony and collapsed to the ground.

"Sneaky cunt," snarled Smith raising the entrenching tool to deliver a finishing blow. Webb was in too much pain to even make a futile defence with his hands. Suddenly, Smith's head exploded in spray of blood and bone. Vukasin's bullet had found its mark this time. Smith's almost headless torso thudded to the ground and there was silence.

***

Prey, you hadn't hunted alone for a while, but you needed to keep the hunting skills honed, didn't want to go rusty. Old, slow animals, the dull-witted, got picked off easily. Old animals that could no longer hunt with the pack went rogue and began picking off easy prey. They were opportunists, taking what they could, when they could. A bit like a dingo – that's what they were calling you now, the esteemed gentlemen and women of the press. Not very original really, corny you might say, but you couldn't help feeling a little tinge of pride in being awarded your own moniker.

Sometimes you worried it was getting a bit easy. The prey seemed to be getting more docile. It was their lack of common sense that made you laugh the most. Their herd-like affinity with each other, their slavish devotion to electronic gizmos making it seem like they had abdicated part of their existence to cyberspace. The result of this electro-Faustian pact meant they moved in an ether of information but without the cognitive skill to assemble its mass into any discernible shape or put it into verbal or written form with any skill or dexterity. But this was all grist to the mill; you had a reputation to maintain. It was time to hunt; perhaps you'd take a live one and have a little fun this time. You've got an idea you want to try out, a little old school, but it should work. You've also found a great way of capturing those key moments. Technology might have its drawbacks, but it was amazing what you could film with a phone these days…

# Fullilove ranch, Brayford River Valley, Northern Territory.

Terry Fullilove's place had never seen so much action. His bedroom had been requisitioned for the cop, James; his stock-woman, Natalie and her boyfriend, Clive took the spare room. All three had been brought in with the convoy of police vehicles, a mixture of crew cab Hiluxes and Land Cruisers.

Both men had been stretchered through his living room, conscious but looking dazed. James was covered in burned clothes and dried blood, his left arm hanging limply at his side. The medics had cut away his burnt clothes, swabbed, sutured and stitched. After an hour or so he'd looked human again, clad in a pair of Fullilove's monogrammed pyjamas. He'd been hooked up to a saline drip to counter the effects of dehydration.

For Natalie, a shower, change of clothes and a few hours' sleep would see her right.

Clive had been brought in semi-conscious, he been given a shot of morphine to dull the pain of his broken leg. However, the break was clean and he was otherwise in good shape. The medics had splinted the broken femur and put the whole leg in a fibre glass sleeve. "He should be walking again in a few months," said the doctor.

"He'll still be crap at football, though," quipped Vukasin.

Fullilove had smiled. *You wouldn't believe that less than twelve hours previously she'd blown somebody's head off,* he thought to himself.

Fullilove had assured her that any medical bills for Clive would be taken care of. Smith's body had been brought in strapped to a stretcher and covered in a blanket. Two uniformed cops bearing shotguns stood guard outside Fullilove's door.

# Chandler Police Station, Northern Territory

The NT Police Commissioner was in a sombre mood. He sat in his shirt sleeves, his tie askew, and the smell of beer on his breath. His dress uniform jacket hung on the back of a chair and his bush hat and gloves sat on his desk. He had just returned from the funeral of Howard Chatwin.

The 22-year-old had been on front-line duty less than six months when Tyler Smith had shot him dead in cold blood. The flap of his holster containing his service weapon had not even been undone when his body had been removed from the burnt-out Land Cruiser. His wife and parents had not been allowed to see the body before the coffin had been sealed. Not that what was inside bore much resemblance to her husband or their son anyway.

The Commissioner had uttered a heartfelt and moving tribute to the young officer, but now as he sat alone in his office, the words he uttered sounded cheap and mealy-mouthed. Over two hundred uniformed officers had lined the street to the Catholic Church. Six of Chatwin's colleagues, who had graduated with him in the same year, bore his coffin. The usual ritual of firing a volley was forgotten in the light of the manner in which he had met his death, but whatever the rights and wrongs, however grand the rituals and trappings were, putting a twenty-two-year-old in the ground was not something the Commissioner had ever wanted to do. Lampeter and Fenwick had also received funerals with full honours.

# Sheraton Hotel, Melbourne, Victoria.

It seemed like several lifetimes ago that Lawrence James had left Melbourne. It might have only been a few weeks since he'd left the city on a coach, but a lot had happened in that short time.

The drop in temperature and the bustle and noise of a metropolitan city left him suffering from a little culture shock. Not that he'd had time for much; his three-man security detail had escorted him all the way back on the specially chartered executive jet. Once at the airport he'd been told to put on a bulletproof vest and had been whisked away in a people carrier with blacked-out windows.

He was digesting all that had occurred in the last few weeks as he lay on his king-size double bed in the Sheraton Hotel. He was cocooned in a suite on the top floor which had been requisitioned for the duration of Bain's trial; the jury were also to be accommodated on this floor. A separate lift which opened into the subterranean parking garage made it an ideal venue for such a task. Three teams of six officers kept guard. On the roof a two-man sniper team had been posted. No chances were being taken.

James was lying on his bed clad only in his boxer shorts and shirt, the breeze from the coast felt fresh after the hot, dusty breezes of the NT. In the distance a tram tolled its bell, acting like a balm to his troubled mind.

On the chair hung his best suit and a fresh sling for his wounded arm. He didn't need it but the prosecution had said it would add weight to the idea of an officer wounded in the line of duty. Anything that would send Bain down for a stretch was okay by him.

What he really did want was a cigarette; he couldn't exactly go and get some from the nearest seven-eleven, though.

The word from informants was that Bain had put a half-million-dollar bounty on his head. Ironic, really, when you thought he was the one cooped up here surrounded by armed guards. There were no bars, admittedly, but there might as well have been. Perhaps he could cadge a smoke from one of his bodyguards. *Time to get suited and booted,* he thought, moving from the bed to the chair.

# Police Headquarters, Melbourne.

Cyrus Bain's eyes were still smarting as he was roughly manhandled out of the dark of a holding cell into the bright sunlight of a Melbourne day and into the rear of an unmarked black Range Rover. The two-tonne vehicle had the speed and weight to get away from or crash through most hairy situations. An escort car with four detectives carrying automatic weapons was to follow. Bain was clad in a cheap suit like his escorts, all identical with the exception that his hands were cuffed behind his back. He'd not had any food since the evening when a tray of cold pasta had been thrust into the cell.

At 3am that morning the lights had gone on, angry voices had shouted, "Stand up now!"

He'd done as he was told. The door had opened and a jet of captor spray had hit him full in the face. Instantly his eyes had begun streaming, snot filled his nose and he struggled for breath. Not that he'd had time to think about it. Two or three men, he figured, crashed in and stomped him. Boot kicks had rained down on him for a minute or so and then the door had slammed shut and the lights had gone off.

He'd lain there, blinded and choking for an hour, drenched in his own piss. A particularly deft kick to his kidneys had caused him to lose control.

In the showers that morning he'd inspected the damage. They'd known what they were doing and there wasn't a mark on his face or hands.

A burly cop pushed his head down and into the back seat of a Range Rover. The cop followed him and the door slammed

The two cars sped off; the cop to his left pulled out his Glock 17 and jammed it painfully into Bain's ribs.

"If we're held up for even a second too long at a traffic light or a bike gets too close for comfort I'm gonna shoot you in the fucking base of the spine. Get it?" the cop snarled. "I'm not gonna shoot you in the head, it'd be too quick and make a mess of my mate's suit."

Bain remained impassive, but he was impressed by the originality of the threat.

The cars sped on into the city centre. A media scrum had begun two hours before the trial was due to begin. TV cameramen and photographers jostled for space outside the court. The old hands had been there the night before and padlocked their stepladders to the railings, ensuring a ringside seat. A couple of news anchors checked their hair and make-up; men and women. A queue of people eager to get a position on the public gallery snaked round the corner as they and their possessions were put through airport style security scanners.

Outside, the air suddenly filled with the sound of sirens. The TV cameras quickly panned to the roof of the opposing building where an eagle-eyed reporter had spotted the sniper teams deployed on the roof. A convoy of vehicles appeared. Two police motorcycle outriders blocked the road junction halting the traffic as two marked police cars blasted through the intersection closely followed by a prison van and another marked car. The electronic gates rolled back and swallowed the convoy. A cordon of uniformed police officers surged forward to stop overzealous photographers from getting through the gap.

Defendant and key prosecution witness alike had been brought in via the subterranean entrance of the court, well away from the circus at the front of the court. Bain was pushed into a small holding cell with two officers taking up station outside the steel door. James was taken to a small, stuffy, windowless room where witnesses waited their turn to take the stand. The first day of the trial would be taken up with the opening statements of the opposing counsels and a final bout of horse-trading over which order the witnesses should take the stand. Bain would be brought up into the dock to confirm his identity and then taken back to the cells. Given the security concerns, the public gallery had been cleared and the press bench had been restricted to five journalists who had drawn lots to get a place in the pool. All copy was to be syndicated, much to the chagrin of the competitive journos: sharing and mutual co-operation were not words in their professional vocabulary.

The city authorities had wanted Bain to appear in court via a video link, but the Chief Commissioner was having none of it.

Bain would not be holding the authorities to ransom; the city was no longer his fiefdom. When he was successfully convicted Bain would be sent to a jail in Western Australia where his tentacles had not spread; or at least as so far as current intelligence could confirm. This was the trade-off with the authorities the Chief Commissioner had made to get Bain brought to stand in the dock in person. But he knew they would be back for their pound of flesh.

Day one of the highest profile criminal trial Melbourne and the State of Victoria had seen for years rumbled to a close. The key protagonists returned to their cell or confinement in a hotel room.

The number of fans for "Cyrus Bain is an Aussie legend" Facebook page stood at just over 5,000. This fan page had grabbed the attention of Fiona Hawkins, news anchor for Oceania News, the state's most watched news channel and the current hot ticket channel for the city's youth.

Hawkins had come across the page whilst surfing the internet at her desk. She had grabbed a low-fat bagel and a skinny latte from the plush coffee bar in the atrium of the glass and steel cube that played host to Oceania News. She was waiting for her hair stylist, prior to presenting the lunchtime "news blast" – three minutes of top news from the city. The programme lasted just about as long as the attention span of the channel's key stakeholders (or viewers, in old money).

Despite having been selected for her job on the strength of her winning Miss Melbourne six years previously, Hawkins wanted to be taken seriously and fostered ambitions that went well beyond the length of her perfectly crafted nails. She wanted to be seen as a journalist, not as "news eye candy", as her less than politically correct editor had called her. Nonetheless, she had found another angle, something that would put the jaded old hack in her shadow, where he belonged. She picked up her phone and dialled the number of a friend who worked with young offenders in a less salubrious area of the city.

"Joanne, it's Fi here, I have an angle on this Bain trial. If it works, it'll be to both our benefits. Can we do lunch tomorrow?"

# Northern Territory Police HQ, Darwin.

Back in the Northern Territory, Adrian Marsh had got nothing but an aching back and legs as a reward from a morning's graft in the basement of police headquarters.

The main archive had been scanned to microfilm and the originals moved to a secure warehouse after 1974, when Cyclone Tracy had devastated Darwin. However, as part of Operation Nemesis, a review of previous files related to The Dingo Case had been ordered and so these documents had been boxed up and trucked back to their original basement home. It was here now that Marsh had spent the morning toiling through witness statements, police reports, interview transcripts and the numerous other documents which accrue during a major investigation.

Civilians weren't normally allowed access to police archives, especially the archives of active investigations. But Marsh had been given special dispensation via a request from James, who had vouched for him.

He took the lid off a box – this was more like it. Logs from roadblocks around the time of the first Dingo murders. He pulled out an armful of documents and placed them on the Formica-topped table, which was otherwise empty save for an angle-poise lamp. Marsh sat down, turned on the lamp and began to read. It was going to be a long day.

# Melbourne Law Courts.

Day three of the highest profile case Melbourne had seen for decades, the crowds and the media scrum had died away.

But inside Court Number One, the drama was just ratcheting up. For this was the day when the defendant and the key prosecution witness were to come face-to-face. The prosecution had decided to take the gloves off and press for an attempted murder charge instead of the lesser charge of grievous bodily harm. Their choice was simple: with the attempted murder charge came the inevitability of a mandatory life sentence. Bain would serve at least fifteen years before being considered for parole. It would be a slam dunk for the cops and prosecutors. Either way they thought Bain being sent down was inevitable. This lay due to their twin track policy: they had held back all the charges of racketeering, tax evasion and living off immoral earnings for now.

The police had played an excellent counter-surveillance operation by having it put around via informers and others that the charges had been dropped due to lack of evidence. This was far from the case. They had simply kept their proverbial powder dry. There was another sting in the tail waiting for Bain and his coterie of lawyers. To prevent leaks from the Victoria Prosecutor's Office, the charges were being brought by prosecutors from the State of New South Wales. A number of sample offences had been allegedly committed there allowing them to bring the prosecution case. If Bain walked free on the attempted murder charge he'd simply be rearrested by Victoria cops on the steps of the court on a New South Wales warrant and carted off to Sydney. The likelihood of absconding on serious fraud charges meant he would be held in custody.

This is not to say that Bain's lawyers were simply going to lie down and play dead. Far from it, like cornered animals, they had fought back more viciously than ever before, albeit with sheaves of paperwork rather than tooth and claw. The central plank of their legal defence was that the state of Victoria had pursued a reckless and ruthless personal vendetta against Cyrus Bain, a legitimate businessman who was going about his business. They argued that the raid had been staged on the flimsiest of evidence. Bain had simply been defending his property against what he thought were intruders.

At the case conference that morning the defence team had taken heart at the climbing numbers joining Bain's Facebook group, currently topping 7,000 members. The press had also got hold of the story – the Melbourne quality broadsheet, *The Age*, running a profile of Bain entitled "Cyrus Bain – Melbourne's 21st century Ned Kelly?".

In the courtroom, Bain was brought in that morning flanked by four hefty security guards. He was, however, clad in an immaculately tailored bespoke suit and sported a two-hundred-dollar haircut. His lawyers had successfully argued that being dressed in prison issue clothes visually represented him to the jury as implicitly guilty.

James appeared in the witness box after two police witnesses had put in a stellar performance. In the morning's proceedings, James was questioned about his previous police record and his involvement with the Armed Offender's Squad and its acrimonious ending. James stepped down from the witness box thinking he'd acquitted himself quite well, when his ex-colleague Jim Davenport was called to the stand.

Bad blood was an insufficient form of expression for the visceral hatred the two men shared. While Davenport's performance was only mediocre it served its purpose, to raise questions about James' integrity just as he was due to take the stand that afternoon as the prosecution's main witness. After all, he was the one Bain had shot.

The judge and jury adjourned for lunch. Bain was returned to his cell feeling a little more optimistic than he had at the start of the morning session.

James, meanwhile, brooded and began plotting revenge of a less legitimate kind on Davenport who had raised his ire to fever pitch.

# Clifton Street, Melbourne.

Across the city, two pretty, young, glamorous women were enjoying a convivial lunch in an equally glamorous restaurant. The Gilded Lily was the current flavour of the month for the city's cognoscenti and had received rave reviews in *The Age*. Hawkins' media credentials had secured her a table, while Joanne Frampton had credentials of her own that secured top-notch service and attentive staff. Over their Caesar salads and bottled water, the two women shared their latest indiscretions and office dalliances.

Hawkins' latest conquest had been a runner at the studios who had been on a week-long internship. The fifteen-year age gap had not bothered either of them.

Frampton was nominally married to a rich hedge fund manager who usually put in seventy hours a week at the office, only requiring her obedience as trophy wife at Melbourne society events and charity fund-raisers. Her latest piece of fun, she said, "was a bit of rough, a silver fox" but she couldn't name names because "he was connected in dubious circles". It was only when they ordered their post-lunch double espressos that the conversation turned to the ostensible purpose of their meeting.

"So, your twist on my idea, why do you think linking up with a major crim like Bain will help New Directions?" asked Hawkins. New Directions was the charity that Frampton ran and was one which her husband's hedge fund "chucked the odd mill at" – and worked with young adults in crime-ridden neighbourhoods who were considered "at risk" of becoming offenders. It was no coincidence that these same neighbourhoods were fertile recruiting grounds for Bain's cohorts.

"Well it's not so much about him being a major crim, it's what he was *before* he became a crim that we're interested in," said Frampton, toying with an errant piece of celery the waiter had missed when clearing the table.

"I get you, so a sort of heart-to-heart with the city's youth," said Hawkins, her journalistic avarice barely concealed.

"That's it," Frampton replied, casting a discreet eye at the clock on her Blackberry which lay on the table.

"I'll have to clear it with the old goat back at the office, but I'll just unbutton my blouse a few buttons and give him the full broadside," smiled Hawkins, jiggling her more than ample breasts to emphasise her intentions. Both women shared a laugh and got up to leave. Hawkins' bill had been paid for on her business credit card. Frampton's had simply been placed on the table stamped as "paid in full". Both women rose from the table, replaced various items in their handbags and hugged, departing with promises to meet "ASAP" again.

Hawkins clip-clopped through the marble foyer to her chauffeured car. Frampton lingered in the entrance and took a pack of Winfield Light cigarettes from her crocodile-skin handbag. She had just lit her cigarette and was inhaling the smoke gratefully, when her mobile phone beeped. The words "Nail Technician" showed who was calling, but behind the façade, it was her piece of rough, aka Dave Spinks, Bain's éminence grise.

# Melbourne Law Courts.

The trial resumed for the afternoon session. James took the witness stand and began his testimony regarding the day he met Bain in the corridor of the house.

Bain's counsel had probed, blustered and grandstanded, trying to irk James into slipping from the narrative.

James had practised his performance the night before, pacing the floor of his hotel room wearing only his boxer shorts and clutching a glass of Johnnie Walker Red on the rocks. Thus, like a Roman legion or a Greek phalanx, James had stood firm under the torrent of legalese.

Back in the UK, James had faced QCs in his time so was not overly impressed by Bain's lawyer. In James' view, hiring this guy to defend him had been the first mistake he'd seen Bain make. Going for the best lawyer money could buy was always a mistake. They were usually past their best, middle-aged, had teenage kids and spent too much time in client meetings and boozy lunches, associated with corporate, not courtroom work. It was better to find a young – but not too young – lawyer who had a few decent victories under their belt but hadn't won the case that would make their name.

At the post-court session debriefing, James and the prosecution team chalked the day up as an away draw in football terms.

# Cooper's Cross, Northern Territory.

Felicity Campbell sat with her feet stretched out in front of her, her milk-white ankles peeping out from the gap between her pedal pushers and ankle socks, slung low in scuffed Vans skater shoes.

The tinny sound of a song emanated from her white headphones. On the table next to her in a stubby cooler sat a half-drunk beer, Victoria Bitter, or "tourist pop" as the locals dubbed it.

An iPhone lay on the table next to her, intermittently pinging as emails were received. There'd been a slew of them since she'd spent yesterday morning in an internet café uploading pictures to Facebook. They had been of her fortnight in Melbourne; parties, early mornings to bed, up late in the mornings. She'd decided to visit the NT at the last minute when she'd met a Dutch girl who'd bagged one of two really cheap flights left to Darwin. She hadn't needed much persuading. They had travelled around the sites of Darwin, amazed at the resilience of a city that seemed to emerge time after time from the natural and man-made disasters which had devastated it.

Her Dutch friend's enthusiasm had waned however when Felicity had said she wanted to see the "real outback" Her friend skipped out and instead booked on a two-day Harley Davidson Uluru Experience.

Felicity, slightly narked but nonetheless not discouraged, got a lift with three other women down the Stuart Highway and parted company with them at Dally Waters. Her plans were so far unclear but at this juncture they definitely involved writing some postcards home and swigging another beer.

She had clocked the fifty-something man sitting at the opposite table. It was peculiar, the way he kept on reaching for a large, almost comic-sized handkerchief and blowing his nose, especially in the bright blazing sunlight of a Northern Territory day. She'd heard of summer colds, and surmised that wherever there were people there were germs, thus colds. It reminded her of the cold, damp and woefully short winter days when she had been working as an office temp in London. She had commuted from her home in Reading, twenty-five minutes and a whole world away from London. She had left her parent's comfortable detached house in the Reading suburbs at silly o' clock and got back mid-evening, having braved the jam-packed commuter train and the crammed tube.

She picked up her iPod and scrolled through her tracks. She selected "Down in the Tube Station at Midnight" by The Jam and took another swig of her beer. The lyrics and Paul Weller's flat tones made her think of her parents and their routine of retired life, mowing lawns, shopping at Waitrose, washing the car. Those early mornings had been worth it, though. Here she was, off the tourist trail, alone, but with money and happy. Her concentration was broken as she realised the handkerchief man was standing near her, all her sense of inbuilt British propriety came flooding back.

"'Down in the Tube Station at Midnight', excellent track," said the man with an easy smile.

"I'm sorry, I'll turn it down," she said reaching for the iPod.

"No, it's fine, it's so nice to hear someone listening to such good music, I get bored rigid of hearing AC/DC and mullet rock over here," he added with a wry grin.

Her tension evaporated as quickly as it had arrived. Then she did something she had never done since school, something she'd never had done on the tube or at home. She unhooked a headphone, proffered it to the man and said, "Here, be my guest if you want to listen for a bit."

Perhaps she never should have.

# Roper Valley, Northern Territory.

Under the same burning sun, Adrian Marsh had pushed the car's air-conditioning up to max. He was on the way to see an old friend, well, not so much an old friend as an acquaintance. He was hot from the sun, but also he felt an inner burning, the kind you get in your gut, when you know you're onto something good. For all their mutual loathing, cops and journos shared this same fixation. It was the one that made you forget all the other things in life and sometimes ended in Pulitzers and plaudits, but more often than once, when the bill came to be paid for all the late nights and broken promises, it ended in divorce and despair. Nevertheless, when you had drunk from this well, no water ever tasted sweeter and the desire for it never left you.

Marsh was on the way to see Murray Sutton, a retired NT cop. Sutton lived on an old broken-down ranch in the Roper Valley. Like Marsh he'd inherited it from a relative. He'd been making decent efforts at raising cattle until one day, when he'd been forking out hay for his young stock, he had coughed up some blood. A round of tests told him he had progressive lung cancer; he'd got six to eight months. He was confined to the house and received thrice-weekly visits from a nurse who delivered drugs and basic essentials.

Marsh left the Roper Highway and drove up a blacktop service road. Sutton's house sat at the bottom of a series of buildings which formed a U-shape. The cattle sheds looked empty and forlorn, bereft of their livestock. Only a pile of part-used cattle feedbags gave an inkling of what once had been here. The house was an expansive homestead with verandas on all sides, the window blinds were all drawn. "And each slow dusk, a drawing-down of blinds," murmured Marsh to himself, feeling slightly like an impostor, clutching the bottle of whisky and hardback edition of *The Complete Stories of Sherlock Holmes*. A wolf in sheep's clothing bearing symbols of friendship but with an ulterior motive.

"The guy's fucking dying, he's not going to give a fuck why I'm here, he's just going to be glad to see someone," said Marsh to himself as he crossed the yard and went through the screen door, leaving any qualms there. Having received no answer after knocking the interior door, Marsh made his way into the darkened interior. That was when he became aware of the hissing and gurgling noise from the next room. He bristled with fear, but advanced cautiously into the next room, his grip on the bottle of whisky tightening. His apprehension quickly gave way to horror and pity as he gazed upon the wreck of a man that Murray Sutton had become.

The huge bulk of a man had shrunken to a shadow of himself; stick-thin. He was clad in pyjamas and dressing gown. Over his face was an oxygen mask whose tube linked to a metre-high oxygen cylinder, the source of the gurgling.

The bird-like man shuffled and said in a rasping voice; "Bloody hell it's the journo of Christmas past. Bearing gifts, too. You must want something?" said Sutton. His body might be dying, but his mind was as sharp as ever.

Marsh was going to have his work cut out.

"Shut your cake-hole and pour the booze. Then you can tell me what you want," Sutton said with a wheezy chuckle.

Marsh twisted the cap off the whisky and sloshed a liberal measure into two tumblers he had found on the sideboard. Marsh took the opportunity to take in the surroundings. Despite the austere furniture, the room was very well appointed. There was a relatively new large plasma screen television and a Bang and Olufsen stereo next to a sideboard well stocked with single malt whisky and an assortment of other spirits.

"Had a win on the horses?" asked Marsh, picking up a framed picture of a sun-tanned, good-looking couple in their thirties with their arms wrapped around two young children. The picture had been taken at Disney World in Florida.

"Let's say some of my investments came good. Apart from the fact that my lungs are being destroyed at a rate of knots, life's just peachy," said Sutton, who had removed his facemask to take a swig of whisky.

"So you cashed in your investments to live a little of the good life before you fall off your perch," said Marsh, sipping his whisky.

"Well, there's not much future for me, is there? It's the kids I want to help out and see them enjoy themselves before they put me in the ground," said Sutton.

"Well, it's the past I've come to talk about. More to the point, about a certain time at a certain roadblock, when a certain car appeared and a certain copper happened to recognise the make, model and owner, and yet twenty years later the record seems to have disappeared," said Marsh.

Sutton trembled and his left hand shuddered, rocking the table next to him and causing the plethora of inhalers and pill bottles on it to shudder.

"Wow, you don't mess about, do you?" said Sutton.

"There's somebody out there who's picking off young girls, one by one. Whatever you know can't be more important than that. It's always going to come down to someone ripping someone off or someone shagging someone else," growled Marsh.

"Okay, okay, I getcha," wheezed Sutton.

"So what's it going to be?"

"Whaddya mean?" asked Sutton.

"Well it's like this. Either 285138 Staff Sergeant Sutton tells me what happened on the night of 24th September 1995 and you die everybody's favourite grandpops or they get to put you in the ground knowing you're a lying scumbag who refused to help in a murder enquiry. Either way, I don't give a fuck. The choice is yours," said Marsh.

Sutton raised his hands in surrender. "All right, but what I'm gonna tell you stays with you for your use and then goes six feet under with me. You don't make any recordings or write anything down. I've got dough coming to me that'll keep coming after I'm worm food. I know I've made some cack-handed decisions, but muck-raking won't change anything. That's the deal," said Sutton.

***

It had gone like clockwork; you had to give yourself a pat on the back for this one. It's like Abduction 101, so audacious, yet so simple. Chloroform, just crowbarred a door at the back of a photography studio and job done. Walking along watching the sunset over the outback, at the end of a street. She'd been staring at it when you grabbed her from behind and clamped your handkerchief over her mouth. She'd collapsed into your arms like a newborn foal taking its first, faltering steps. You'd piled her under a hoodie and gone to get the van. You'd put an empty bottle of beer next to her, so she'd look like she'd passed out after one too many.

A few minutes later you'd driven out of town unobstructed. A piece of cake. The hunter with the prey. On the stereo... "Comfortably Numb".

# Melbourne Law Courts.

The end game came swiftly. After the pageant, bluster, grandstanding, argument and counterargument of the previous seventeen days, Judge Martin Hackett put a final full-stop to the preceding days of dialogue. "Cyrus Bain, you have been found guilty by a jury of your peers. Attempting to kill one of the Queen's Police officers with malice aforethought means I have no qualms in sentencing you to the maximum sentence it is at my discretion to hand down. You will go to prison for twenty-five years, with no eligibility for parole for at least fourteen years. You are a clear and present danger to the people of Melbourne and the State of Victoria. I have no doubt that your incarceration will make the streets of our city a safer place to live. Take him down."

A roar erupted outside the courtroom as news of the verdict and subsequent sentence reached the small but vocal mob of Bain's supporters who howled their outrage. An outpouring which was soon drowned out by the wail of sirens.

The thin cordon of uniform officers hemming them in retreated under a volley of plastic chairs and beer bottles. A plume of orange flame erupted as an outside broadcasting van from one of the television news channels was pelted with Molotov cocktails. Retribution was swift, however. A convoy of police vans, wire mesh guards down over their windscreens, pulled to a halt and disgorged a number of black-clad officers equipped with riot shields and batons. Forming a wedge they began to carve a swathe through the young men who threw anything they could. Minimum force was put to one side in the melee.

A man in his thirties raised a plastic chair, a baton hit him in the back of the legs and he sank to the floor. As he tried to stagger to his feet, a cloud of captor spray hit him in the face. He clutched his hands to his face, screaming in pain. His screams were soon stymied as a volley of baton strokes smashed into his head and torso. Blood spumed from his nose as it broke. His beaten and battered body was dragged through the front lines of the riot cops leaving a slick of blood and mucus on the asphalt. Bain's cohorts were soon splintered and broken.

For the two main protagonists, one's incarceration would soon be ended, the other's was now to be defined by a number of days, weeks and years until he could put himself forward for parole. Bain had played the "not guilty" card and come out the loser. If he'd have put his hands up to shooting James, he would have gotten maybe ten years, with a possibility of parole after five.

But this was not what was irking him. He'd played his hand and lost, he'd been phlegmatic enough about that. But the piece of news that had floored him was delivered with his breakfast, with its usual nutritional addition of warder spit.

For the duration of his sentence, Bain was property of the state correction services; in this instance, the state of Victoria. However, the letter informed him, that due to internal investigation and pending prosecutions which pertained to him, he would be spending the foreseeable future in the care of the Western Australian Department of Corrections, namely in Freemantle jail.

*Tess,* thought Bain and exploded. "Cunts! Absolute cunts," howled Bain. He upended his tray full of food and began kicking the steel door of his cell.

The final paragraph of the letter had revealed that his two-year-old daughter would be taken into the adoptive custody of the state, after his incarceration and her mother's continuing alcohol dependency.

An alarm sounded and the Crash Response Team entered Bain's cell, batons drawn, ready to mete out some retribution for the rejection of their hospitality. They were to be disappointed. Bain slumped on the floor, holding his hands forward in supplication, as they slipped the handcuffs on. They led him to an isolation cell, where he would be under twenty-four-hour supervision. He lay meekly on the bunk as a prison medic gave him a sedative injection and he subsided into a peaceful slumber.

The arm of Bain's apparent nemesis, Lawrence James, ached. It was not from being shot, but from raising his arms aloft in jubilation when the verdict and sentence was read out.

James had been in a spartan back office of the court accompanied by three armed plain clothes officers and the ceiling had been low.

Bain was secured in the cells at Police HQ and the clean-up teams were hosing the blood and detritus from the pavements after the pitched battle outside the court.

James was allowed to leave. He had made a brief appearance at the spontaneous party which had broken out in The Purple Turtle, a bar frequented by many cops in the city. After swigging a couple of beers, he had made his excuses and left.

His room at the Sheraton was still booked for the rest of the week. His bodyguards had been whittled down to three armed detectives each taking an eight-hour shift. James would have this protection until the end of the week when he was due to fly back to the NT.

James had gone back to his room, secretly relieved he had been able to get away from the formality of the court and the boozy bonhomie of his colleagues. He took off his jacket, stooped down and opened the mini bar. He extracted a miniature of Johnnie Walker Red Label, and poured it into a tumbler. He paused, made a silent toast to the memories of his fellow officers, Lampeter, Fenwick, Chatwin and the pilot, Curtis. He downed the drink and then lay down on the bed, falling into the first decent sleep he'd had in two months.

# Roper Valley, Northern Territory.

"So The Brotherhood wasn't just bullshit, then?" said Marsh. An hour and a half had gone by since the two men had cut their deal. The bottle of whisky was two-thirds empty. In the interim Sutton had outlined a decade-long odyssey of brown envelopes left on desks, cruises paid for and mortgages paid off, along with the tawdry details of what these bagatelles had pardoned. Mostly run-of-the-mill stuff, parking offences, drink-driving, but also more serious things that been harder to stomach; things that attracted a few years in jail and had been papered over. Things Marsh had sworn to look the other way about, either way.

"Yes, that's the nub of it. All these things stemmed from The Brotherhood: A bunch of guys who had most of the cops, councillors, clerks and politicians in their pockets," said Sutton, breaking into a hacking coughing fit.

The Brotherhood had been the stuff of legend when Marsh had been a cub reporter on *The Darwin Telegraph*. Rumours had swirled about the whole NT, about this shadowy organisation that permeated every level of the state, with its sticky fingers in every pie. If a new highway was being built or a juicy renovation project beckoned, it always seemed to breeze through any oppositions, with planning consent a given and the contract invariably awarded to one of the cartel allegedly involved with The Brotherhood who were always sticking their boards up outside the new building sites or other construction projects.

With the benefit of hindsight, Marsh could pinpoint an episode when he crossed paths with one of the tentacles of this elusive kraken. Late one night he'd been in the newsroom putting a feature to bed on the increase in cattle rustling in the NT when the phone rang. It was a tip-off from a friendly cop that a senator had been pulled in and arrested for knocking down a twelve-year-old boy in Renner Springs while out of his head on booze. Marsh was on his way to leave the office when the phone had rung. It had been his editor, Baz Twomlow.

"The senator is going to make amends, so don't bother going to the station. He'll be released without charge. See you tomorrow." The phone had gone dead.

Marsh had just become a father, he had a young wife, a mortgage and he was dog-tired. He wouldn't have rocked the boat even if he had put the pieces together there and then. The words came back to him: *He'll be*, not *he'll probably be*. Marsh remembered the kid. He'd been a bright kid from a poor stock farming family. But fortune, it seemed, had smiled on him. For his leg fractured in two places and his family's silence he'd made it into a top fee-paying school thanks to a special bursary and the same for three years of university. The benign light of The Brotherhood had shone upon him, it seemed.

"So that's the bigger picture stuff, but to be specific about that roadblock – it's pretty sketchy, but I've got enough to put you up another ladder," said Sutton. "Well, it was a shitty rainy night. The Dingo had knocked off his fifth victim and was ripping the piss out of us, sending us letters and calling the detectives working on the case in the middle of the night. Well, there was me, I had made Staff Sergeant, Jim Ferguson and Andy Wilson, he'd just qualified out of the academy. We'd been told to stop all the traffic coming along the Stuart Highway just down the road from Boxwood Police station.

"I was sitting in the car and radioing back the details as the other two collected the licence plates and descriptions. These were then being typed up and fed into the database back in Darwin. We'd rigged up some flashers and had blocked one lane of the blacktop with some oil barrels. Wilson was waving cars down with a flashlight and taking down details, Jim Ferguson was training a twelve-gauge on the cars, covering Wilson and ready to shoot them or the car's tyres if they pulled a gun or made a run for it. We'd started at 7pm that evening, there'd been a few road trains, a few camper vans, and we'd taken a few ounces of weed off some tourist kids – in exchange for the contents of their wallets and all their traveller's cheques. I think we made about three hundred bucks, 'toll bonus' we called it," said Sutton with a chuckle and a wry smile.

Marsh did not reciprocate.

"So, it gets to three in the morning and I've dozed off when there's a knock on the car door. Wilson's in a hell of a state, 'Boss, we've got a problem up here, I think you better come quick,' he says. So I get out and follow him. There's a guy spread-eagled across the bonnet of a fancy car, Ferguson's got him cuffed and is sticking his revolver in the guy's neck. 'Bastard tried to fob me off with some sob story about being late back from a funeral and then tried to burn off, so I slotted him', said Ferguson, jabbing his gun into the guy's neck." Sutton had a distant look in his eyes.

"So I got Ferguson off him, put the suspect in my car and drove him to the station. I stuck him in the cells, booked him in with the duty sergeant and got back to the roadblock. That's when things got weird.

"I'd just poured myself a coffee and was splitting up our toll money when the radio crackles. I get told to wrap up the roadblock and bring the other two and the suspect's car back as well.

"When I get there, there's a bloody Superintendent in full war paint waiting for me and I get a roasting. Ferguson has to go and apologise to the guy for roughing him up and a week later he's dismissed for conduct unbecoming a police officer, although he gets a discretionary allowance and a lump sum. He's used it to buy a share in a roadhouse up in Adelaide River. I'll give you his number," said Sutton, standing up and rummaging in a drawer in the sideboard.

"What happened to your paperwork from that night?" asked Marsh. Sutton's recall of the night was good, but a guy in a posh car wasn't going to do much for his investigation, other than confirming his suspicions about there being something extremely suspicious about what should have been a routine event, albeit in extraordinary times regarding the hysteria which had gripped the territory at the time.

"Well I imagine the originals went in the shredder, but I signed a new copy and that went in the files."

"In exchange for thirty pieces of silver, eh?" asked Marsh.

"Suppose so," shrugged Sutton like a teenager who'd been caught smoking.

"Well, I'd better make tracks," said Marsh.

"Here's Ferguson's number," said Sutton, handing Marsh a scrap of paper with a telephone number scrawled on it.

"Thanks," said Marsh.

"You won't miss the place: it looks like a bleeding car museum," said Sutton.

Marsh raised his hand in farewell and left the room.

"See you at the funeral," said Sutton.

Marsh took the service road back to the Roper Highway. His digging had turned over a dung heap and he didn't like the smell. The stink might be old, but the smell still lingered. Older and softer in the middle now some of these guys might be, but they were still shits of the first water.

Marsh was no weepy right-on liberal, but it still stuck in his craw that so many had gotten away with so much, for so long. Nevertheless, a promise was a promise; he had gotten what he wanted, at a price. Marsh also knew he wasn't dealing with mere demons from the past; these apparitions were flesh and blood and were still alive and kicking. The phoney traffic report that Sutton said he'd filed had been absent. Marsh pointed the car home and started making plans for a trip to Adelaide River.

# Nr Chandler, Stuart Highway, Northern Territory.

Jez Walker was busting for a piss. He'd last stopped for a slash a hundred and fifty miles back. He'd stopped at a roadhouse and stocked up on petrol for the drive to Katharine, as well as a bunch of cans of iced coffee. Jez was a rep for a stationery company. He loved stationery and he loved the road. He was also a frustrated writer who'd found his safe and secure teaching job irksome and the constant interruptions of his wife a little cloying.

Most months he cleared more than his teaching salary anyway, which pleased his wife, and the three to four nights a week he spent away from home gave him chance to concentrate on his work *Whitefella on the Road*. It was going to be *On The Road* for Australia.

Jez had been thinking about the finer points of his character's personality, when a baser need began to overpower him. He changed down a gear and indicated that he was pulling off the blacktop, a force of habit, despite having seen no traffic in either direction for an hour or so.

He got out of the car and did a couple of stretches and then windmilled his arms forwards and backwards a few times. He walked behind a clump of spinifex and took a long, lingering piss, splaying his feet as wide as possible to avoid getting piss on his immaculately polished shoes. The baked red earth proved unyielding and soon rivulets of urine had moved from a central pool to form a delta of individual streams. Walker's eye followed its spread across the solid table-top level earth. Suddenly something crossed his eye; a training shoe, he thought, at first.

A tsunami of his piss enveloped it, and he couldn't help but let out a little smirk as it happened. He zipped up and made his way back to the car. He cleaned his hands with alcohol gel; Jez was fastidious with his hygiene. He reached into his glove compartment and pulled out a fresh pack of Marlboro Reds, bereft of the usual health warning and gory pictures but plastered with Arabic writing. The cigarettes were bought for him via Dubai duty free and even after chucking his mate a few dollars for his trouble they were still a snip. His workaday fags were Winfield Lights, but he treated himself to a pack of Marlboro when he was out and about on the road. He ripped the foil off the pack, pulled one out of the first rank and sparked it up. He got out of the car and leant against the bonnet while the nicotine got to its devilish work.

He leant back against the car, feeling the heat of the afternoon sun reaching its zenith and inhaled deeply. He was musing on how in a few minutes he would be zipping along in his air-conditioned cocoon away from this place and this moment would be history, when something prodded a memory.

Out there, some metres away in the bush lay another trainer. The white flash on the side had caught his eye. He threw his cigarette down and ground the butt out under his heel. He edged his way around the first clump of spinifex adjacent to the road and made his way to where he thought he'd seen the trainer lying. His sense of direction was good. He parted another clump and there it was. He bent down and picked it up. It was a Vans skate shoe, small. *Probably a girl's or young woman's*, thought Walker, weighing it in his hand.

"Curiouser and curiouser, eh?" said a man's voice behind him.

Walker shuddered in unrestrained terror and slowly began to turn. Before he quite made it, a flash of light sent him collapsing to his knees and then everything went black.

# Adelaide River, Northern Territory.

The Adelaide River Road House lay on the Stuart Highway adjacent to the Litchfield National Park; this was the beautiful, but less visited cousin of the more popular Kakadu National Park, famous as the setting for the movie *Crocodile Dundee*.

Litchfield attracted a better cut of tourist, so Marsh thought, and whenever he got the desire to do some bush walking this is where he headed for. Being on the main haul to Darwin meant the Adelaide Road House got a lot of passing trade and Jim Ferguson got a fair amount of cash ringing through his till. His original investment in what had been a rundown collection of tumbledown buildings now sprawled several hundred metres along the highway. He had bought a half share in it when it had been on the verge of bankruptcy. Mainly because Mike Wooldridge was drinking the profits, not through lack of trade.

Now it boasted a beer barn, a fast food restaurant a mini market, a filling station, half a dozen motel rooms and hook-ups and facilities for motor homes.

The centre of this hub of activity was The Crazy Horse tavern, a hybrid of traditional Aussie pub and sixties US diner. At one end was a bar with beer taps and a host of other bottles and drinking paraphernalia. Postcards from previous visitors, and small denomination notes from across the world, were pinned up all over the walls. At the other end a converted railway car had been built into the structure of the building. A waist-high counter complete with spinning vinyl covered stools ran along its length. Half a dozen vinyl booths made up another side. At the far end, the crowning glory was a fifties American juke box, loaded with forty-fives of Elvis, Buddy Holly, The Big Bopper and others. This was Ferguson's domain and was where Marsh found him.

Ferguson was clad in an apron over an open-necked shirt. He'd weathered the storms of life better than Sutton. He was in his mid-fifties, average height and lean, a hint of iron ringing his black hair. He was busy clearing away the aftermath of the lunchtime rush. Ketchup-slick plates vied with large mugs of half-drunk coffees. The five-dollar Big Bopper Burger and the three-dollar bottomless coffee were famous along both directions of the Stuart Highway. Ferguson looked up from his work as Marsh parked himself on a vinyl stool at the counter.

"Well if it's not old inky fingers himself," said Ferguson with a wry smile. "What can I get you?" he asked Marsh.

"Set me up a coffee and I'll see if I'm going to manage a Big Bopper."

"Sure thing. And what brings you to this bit of the Top End?" asked Ferguson, as he deftly picked up a jug of coffee from a hot plate, poured the scalding black brew into a mug and slid it along the counter to Marsh.

"I've been taking a waltz down memory lane with your old chum, Sutton," said Marsh, picking up the coffee mug, turning the handle towards him, and taking a sip. As always it was hot, strong and tasted great.

"I thought the bastard had bought the farm," said Ferguson, with barely concealed contempt.

"He's been baring his soul to me. He mentioned that you'd be able to help me. About things that go bump in the night."

"I get your drift; you better come in the office," said Ferguson, rubbing the bridge of his nose with the back of his hand.

Marsh picked up his coffee and followed Ferguson out of the diner and through a swing door. Off the corridor Ferguson made a left into an office, boasting a desk, two filing cabinets and chairs. He fell into a big leather chair and Marsh pulled up a wooden chair.

"I thought there'd been rumblings. I've had some previous visitors, not welcome like you, though," said Ferguson, pulling up his shirt to reveal a .38 revolver sticking out of his waistband. "A couple of days ago my house just down the road got ransacked. They busted into my desk in the study and stole all the files I had. They left a strongbox with three grand in it untouched, even though it was open. The uniform who came to take a look said it was probably junkies."

"Funny junkies who leave three grand in cash!" replied Marsh with a smirk.

"I think this was what they were after," said Ferguson, pulling back a crate of full beer bottles to reveal a floor safe. He turned the combination lock a few times and the door sprang open. He extracted a brown manila folder and offered it to Marsh.

"Your car-spotting notes, eh?"

"Exactly. I think they were looking for them; someone seems to have been stirring up the past. I take it you're the wombat who's been digging in the shit pile?" said Ferguson.

"Sure am," said Marsh, opening the file.

"Help yourself, there's a copier in the corridor, I've had my money's worth from them, but I'll be buggered if I'm letting those bastards get their greasy mitts on them."

"Can you tell me more about the car that night?" asked Marsh.

"Sure. I've got some pictures in the file there – it was a Pontiac Firebird, a real beauty," chuckled Ferguson.

"This is all I need, you can go back to busting soap suds," said Marsh sardonically.

"You cheeky bastard!" said Ferguson, standing up and hitching up his trousers to carry the weight of the revolver.

"Thanks, mate, and stay safe," said Marsh, picking up the folder.

"Hold your horses and I'll rustle you up a Big Bopper," said Ferguson.

"I'll take you up on that," said Marsh.

A few minutes later Ferguson returned with a burger in a bun with fries and some salad.

"Thanks. You got a spare minute? Take a pew," said Marsh, tucking into his food.

"That Pontiac, why you so interested in it?" asked Ferguson.

"Well, I think the man who was driving it might be our man," said Marsh, spearing some fries.

"Well, you're going to have a job on."

"Why's that?"

"All the pertinent details have been redacted, even on the files I've given you," said Ferguson.

"Shit," said Marsh.

"I can give you a tip: it was a third generation, built somewhere between 1982 and 1992."

"That's still a shitload of cars."

"Not really, if you think about it. It must have been imported, so there's a trail there. Whittle it down to the NT and you must be in low or single figures. And he must have had it serviced, so look for spare parts imports."

"You know, you might be a burger flipper, but behind that apron, there's still a cop," said Marsh, smiling.

Half an hour later he pulled off the forecourt of the Adelaide Roadhouse with a full tank of gas and enough information to move things forward. The beast burned inside him. He had to get back to the ranch and on a flight to Melbourne.

# Supermax, HM Prison Barwon, Victoria.

The lights were still burning in Bain's cell. He lay on his steel-framed bed looking at the ceiling. The tranquillisers were wearing off and the vortex of rage and frustration he felt had subsided to a dull ache behind his temples. An increasing feeling of tranquillity fell over him. He began to meditate.

He always began the process with the carp pond. This image had been with him since he was fifteen. He'd been on a visit from a Young Offender's Institution to an activity centre on the outside of Melbourne. Part of the day had focussed on meditation and constructive thinking. The session had been held in an outdoor Japanese-themed garden, and the centrepiece had been a pond filled with koi carp and shubunkins. Across the pond was a curved bridge much like the one depicted in Monet's "Waterlilies". It had left Bain transfixed and ever since he'd carried the image with him throughout his life. Back in his duplex apartment in the city, the architect's plans for such a garden lay in a desk drawer ready for the dream to come to fruition on two acres of land outside the city.

Bain's mind cleared and his sense of purpose returned. He had no delusions of grandeur, but he knew that his guys weren't just going to abandon him. They had too much to lose from infighting. Bain had deliberately left it so he had no direct successor. His line of thought was interrupted by the metallic clank of the spy hatch being opened. They had been doing this every fifteen minutes for the last two days.

"Bain, get up, you've got a visitor. Come to the door with your hands raised up behind your back. A false move and you'll get maced."

"Alright, I'll be there, let me just put some lippy on," said Bain with a sneer. He stood up from his bed and moved towards the cell door, stepping backwards with his wrists raised up. A pair of strong hands pushed his wrists together and steel bracelets were snapped around them.

"To what do I owe the honour?" asked Bain.

"Real piece of crumpet. The cuffs are so you keep your paws off her, you lowlife," said the prison guard.

The door opened and he was turned about so his cuffed arms were pushed up towards his back. The guard had him where he wanted and it would only need a slight push to send Bain sprawling to the floor, even fracture Bain's wrists. But Bain knew the game, bide your time, play the game.

On an average day in a Melbourne city street, Fiona Hawkins would have turned a lot of men and women's heads. In the drab, utilitarian confines of a correctional facility, she was a revelation. Shoulder-length red hair framed her intricately-boned face. Porcelain white skin complimented her azure blue eyes. Dressed in a white linen two-piece suit, she was sitting casually with an alligator skin handbag on the Formica-topped table. She looked up and shot Bain a killer smile, that caused even his cold demeanour that he had been assuming in the previous few minutes to melt a little. He'd been convinced that the guards had been taunting him and that a cop, lawyer or state representative awaited him.

"Mr Bain, Fiona Hawkins, Oceania Television," said Hawkins, getting to her feet and offering Bain a manicured hand.

"You'll have to forgive my manners, but my personal assistant insists on me wearing these," said Bain, turning briefly.

"Cuffs stay on at all times, miss, make sure you keep your hands in sight at all times as well," said the guard as convivially as it was possible to utter such a demand.

"As you wish, Andy. Now give us five minutes, will you," she said, with a turn of her head.

The guard mumbled something and shambled out of the room, the visiting room door clicked in place after him. In those few seconds Hawkins had placed her open bag on the floor under the table. In front of her were an A4 pad and a pencil; no pens allowed. She'd obviously pulled some strings as it was strictly prohibited for a prisoner and visitor to be left alone.

"Mr Bain, thanks for agreeing to this interview. This is a preliminary interview. Once I've gotten some details from you I'll get back to the studio and speak to our producer, Usha. Then we'll agree a date when we can return with the cameras."

Bain had not agreed to any interview, but he was out of his cell, speaking to a pretty woman, life was looking up. His instincts told him that someone higher up had pulled strings for this situation to have occurred: it was no random turn of events.

Plus, even if he got pushed straight back in the cell, he had two nuggets of information: the layout of the isolation block in relation to the main prison and the name of the prison guard. It was no coincidence that State Correctional Officers wore only their surnames on their uniforms. Andy possibly had a girlfriend, wife or possibly children. For sure, he had a mother and father somewhere. Bain felt his mental powers returning, a cerebral surge.

Hawkins was busily rattling off a number of standard and relatively inane questions, stuff that she could have found out via an internet search any time.

Then it hit him, mentally and physically, a double whammy. She was buying time for what she'd really come to do. This realisation arrived at the same time as he felt the pressure of Hawkins' foot minus its shoe probing his chest area.

Spinks had gambled right when he'd backed the plan. All State Correctional inmates are clad in orange jumpsuits with buttons, metal poppers to be precise. Bain continued to answer the questions, making the answers deliberately expansive.

"I was first sent down for car theft and got six months," he replied.

Her foot had now opened two buttons on his jumpsuit. Hawkins writhed underneath the table, but this movement was imperceptible to the young guard who manned the monitor to which was fed live streaming coverage from the camera strategically placed high in the corner of the room. The red blinking eye of the camera had caused Hawkins a minor tremor at first but she had composed herself quickly. Now for the difficult bit. She had practised the manoeuvre in front of the mirror in her flat last night.

"So, you're facing a lengthy sentence and your assets have been confiscated, how does someone who had everything and now has nothing, cope?" asked Hawkins provocatively.

Her feet grasped the object and moved it from the bag. Clamped between her heels it moved across the space and into the folds of Bain's jumpsuit. She had done it. She placed her feet back on the floor. Bain coughed and moved from side to side slightly. The object slid down into the leg of his jumpsuit. The cell had been cold so the legs of his jumpsuit had been tucked into his sports socks which had elasticated tops, one small victory over the prison authorities. His lawyers had insisted he had Reynaud's syndrome, which left his toes and fingers cold. It would have compromised his human rights to deny him the socks.

Or so the story went.

Hawkins hadn't finished yet though; in more than one way.

The tension of being locked in a room with Bain and the tension of completing the task had left her massively aroused. She moved her feet back towards Bain and began rubbing her feet in his crotch.

Bain's cock went rock hard. It was a revelation for Bain to be in the submissive position where the woman was in control. He couldn't say it was something he disliked.

# Stuart Highway, Northern Territory.

Marsh was motoring along on the Stuart Highway. Dire Straits' "Sultans of Swing" blared from the CD player to drown out the roar of the air-conditioning that was doing its level best to fight the worst of the blazing temperature. Marsh blasted past a branch of Hungry Jack's. A blue car joined the road behind him despite the fact that he was cruising at 120kph, the car which had started as a dot in his rear-view mirror began to close on him.

Marsh dropped his speed to a steadier ninety-five. If the nut-job wanted to go past then he was welcome to. The car got close to Marsh's and pulled alongside. He saw a flash of the driver as the car pulled alongside.

Then there was a sickening crunching and grinding of metal. Marsh felt the impact of the heavier car smash into his car, and felt the wheels slew to the left. He fought to maintain control but it was no use. The car's engine screamed as the wheels hit the verge and slid off the blacktop. Another violent judder went through the car, this time from the rear and this completed the equation.

Dirt and fragments of bushes plumed up over the windscreen as the car bounced off the road and across the red dust for several hundred yards. The terrain broke some of the velocity of the car and it careened into a shallow gully. Marsh had long since shoved his head between his legs and began reciting the Hail Mary. He may have deserted God, but the words came spilling out all the same. There was a flash and bang as the airbag deployed. Marsh slumped forward into its embrace and blacked out.

Marsh awoke to the smell of cordite, where the airbag had gone off. His head ached and his chest hurt. He wiggled his toes and clenched and unclenched his hands into fists, finally he gently moved his head from side to side and then lastly in a gentle circular motion. He pushed the crumpled driver's door to open it, but it wouldn't budge open more than a few inches. "Aircraft style, then," said Marsh. He grabbed his jumper, balled it round his arm and smashed his arm through the glass. The safety glass shattered into a shower of small pieces like balls of hail.

He shimmied through the window, cursing for letting himself become a fat bastard and swearing to cut down on the booze and quit smoking. He lay in the red dust like a floundering fish and got his breath back. Then he sat up and patted himself down, a rustling under his shirt made him stop. He slid under his shirt and it hit the smooth feel of paper. Then he remembered, he had taped the documents around his chest. It was an old trick, but a good one.

Taking a quick look around, his suspicions were confirmed. Fresh tracks followed in the wake of the crazy, veering tracks his car had made as it had careered off the road. Looking around the car he saw the front passenger window had been smashed, pebbles of glass lay on the front passenger seat and in the footwell. The contents of his briefcase which had been locked before he crashed were scattered about.

He picked up his mobile and saw it had gotten cracked during the crash; He went to the boot of the car and grabbed his survival bag. He checked the contents, took two paracetamol out of the small first aid kit and washed them down with a swig of water from one of the litre bottles of water in the rucksack.

Then he slid the battery into his spare mobile phone and waited to see if there was a signal. No dice. He put the phone in his pocket and shouldered the rucksack. He had a long walk to town ahead.

# Nr Chandler, Stuart Highway, Northern Territory.

"Wake up, you sick fuck," said the voice.

Jez Walker heard it through the fog that seemed to swim around his head. A foot jabbed him in the chest and his eyes shot open. A man in shorts and a t-shirt stood over him. His trainer was placed on the centre of Walker's chest; he had a wild look in his eyes and a tremor in his hands, which worried Walker the most, as they were wrapped around a shotgun.

"Don't make a move," the guy repeated, his voice sounding shaky. "You sick fuck, I ought to blast you right here, what have you done to her?" shrieked the man again.

He moved the gun to his right hand whilst fishing his mobile phone from his pocket. Walker's eyes flickered open briefly and then a tide of nausea swept over him and he blacked out once again.

\*\*\*

Bob Welch had been into town to stock up on fencing supplies when he'd seen the white car at the filling station. Not that it had caused him any suspicion then, but when he'd seen the car parked on the verge on the way back an hour later, his suspicions had been aroused. He slowed down to take a look and couldn't see anyone in the car despite the driver's side door being open. He'd travelled on another half a mile or so when his curiosity overwhelmed him and he did a U-turn and drove back. He'd pulled up on the verge a hundred or so yards from the white car and got out. Before he'd got out he'd taken the shotgun he carried for shooting dingoes from the rear of the crew cab and loaded it.

He'd had a run-in with some bikees the previous time when he'd challenged them unarmed. He'd gotten a broken collar bone for his trouble then and wasn't taking any chances today. Walking to the rear of the white car he quickly ascertained it was empty.

Suddenly he had seen movements in the bush to the side of the road. "Hey fella, what's up," he'd shouted but the figure had disappeared into a thicket of spinifex. Welch had lurched into the bushes carrying the shotgun above his head as if wading through a river. He made slow progress towards where he thought he'd seen the man go.

That was when he had fallen over it, or more precisely, her. He'd gone sprawling into the red dust but kept his grip on the gun. He thought it was a rock that had sent him sprawling, but it had been a body. She lay there fully clothed in a foetal position, the whiteness of her ankles and lower legs betrayed the fact that she wasn't local. Her shoes were missing, which had seemed odd. He'd paused to compose himself when he heard something rustling. It had been Jez Walker stirring from his involuntary coma. Welch had gotten a foot and the gun trained on him and called the cops.

\*\*\*

It had been a textbook operation complemented by the bonus of ad hoc opportunism. It had been a risk, but it was one that had been worth taking and one that had paid off. They'd take the sticky-beak in for questioning at least and they'd spend a bunch of time chasing up his background and get bogged down in spurious information. You'd thought that hunting alone would be difficult without her as the honeytrap, but this one had come to you like a moth to a flame. She'd been sweet for a while, but like all of them, once you scratched the surface they were all self-serving little bitches.

The cops had been closing in, especially now you'd found the NT swedeheads had been joined by the headshrinkers from the big city.

This guy would give them something to chew on. She'd been sweet but had to die, you could never leave witnesses, not now, not ever.

# Safehouse, Melbourne.

James had just gotten out of bed and was helping himself to some coffee from a percolator jug in the kitchen of his old colleague, Doug's suburban home when the phone rang.

"Fred Flintstone," said James, in accordance with the prearranged code words whose role was coming in for some mockery hence the juvenile codenames.

"This is Dino. Betty and Wilma will be with you in five," said the male voice.

"Thanks, Dino," said James, replacing the phone on the kitchen wall.

He put his mug of coffee down on the kitchen counter and went into the rear bedroom to get dressed.

It was his third day living the life of a suburban recluse. Doug had rung and offered him the use of his house while he, the wife and kids spent a week in Perth. For James, who'd been climbing the walls of his hotel room, it was simply too good an offer to refuse. He'd phoned his boss and then packed his bag. He simply bought a pair of sunglasses and a tourist baseball cap before joining the throngs of commuters travelling back home to the suburbs.

Sometimes a surging crowd is the simplest and most effective method of counter-surveillance. Plus, since the bomb on the plane, James had suspected there was a leak in the chain somewhere and the fewer people who knew his whereabouts, the better. He'd enjoyed the freedom he'd regained, sleeping in late, going to the nearest 7/11 to grab a paper and some breakfast ingredients and then spending time in Doug's pool. In the evenings he'd watched DVDs in the home cinema accompanied by a bottle of red from the wine cellar. He'd spoken to Sandersen several times by phone, who brought him up to speed on the case.

The doorbell rang. It was Betty and Wilma or, to be more precise, the Chief Commissioner and his press adviser, Maxine Turner. James pressed the remote control on the television and selected the CCTV channel. He saw the two figures standing in front of the camera on the drive outside. He pressed a button on the remote and the gates swung inwards. He picked up his .38 revolver and went to the front door. A quick sweep of the cameras told him it was all clear outside and he opened the door. The door swung open and the Chief Commissioner entered followed by Turner, both of them looking slightly bemused as their gaze fell upon James standing in the hallway, a gun held down at his side.

"Afternoon, sir," said James, with a smirk.

"Jeez, all you need is a white cat and you'll be a bona fide Bond villain," the Chief Commissioner said, returning a smile. "How did you get this technological lair? It's good to see you on form now that scumbag has got his just desserts," he said.

"But it's not all good news," said Turner.

"Okay, but before you hit me with it, can I get you some coffee?" he asked.

"Sure," she replied. "Will it come out of the ceiling or on a monorail?"

"Just from a jug in the kitchen, sadly," replied James.

He disappeared into the kitchen and returned with three steaming mugs of coffee. "Ethiopian, shade grown," he remarked and sat down.

Turner slipped a glossy magazine from her briefcase and placed it on the coffee table.

"*Liquid Pulse* is the new face of magazines for the iPod generation," she said. "And the publication in which Bain is gonna give a warts-and-all interview."

"You're shitting me!" said James, in consternation.

"I'm afraid not," said Turner. "We need to quell the youngsters who are getting hot under the collar and making Bain out as a sort of cross between Ned Kelly and Robin Hood. We need to expose him for what he is and reiterate the fact he's going to spend most of his natural behind bars."

"Who's pulling the strings on this one? I can't see you rolling over for this kind of caper without having one of your hands tied behind your back," said James.

"It's from City Hall. The mayor gets this, we get to send Bain to jail in WA unopposed," said the Commissioner.

"Okay, sounds fair enough," said James taking a swig of coffee, still perceptibly bristling with indignation, "But what's this got to do with me?"

"Well," said the Commissioner. "It's point, counterpoint. One week Bain gets a splash, the bad, the next week you get a splash, the good, we go all out, the wounded cop, etc. What do you think?"

"Well I don't suppose I have much choice if the battle for the hearts and minds of Melbourne's youth is between Bain and me," replied James resignedly. "There's just one caveat," he said fixing his stare on the press officer.

"What's that?" she asked.

"I want Jim Davenport crucified in the media," referring to his no-good weasel of a former colleague.

# City Centre, Melbourne.

Fiona Hawkins had one thing in her life which did not exist merely for her own pleasure or delectation: her three-year-old daughter, Scarlet. The origin of her progeny was, however, as much in line with her lifestyle as her Manolo Blahniks in the walk-in closet or the Modigliani on her apartment walls.

When Fiona had reached her early thirties the murmured conversations which she thought she'd heard in the studio became all too much and she made a secret visit to a fertilisation clinic. Nine months and a natural birth later, Scarlet was born. Circumspection on the origins of the father kept the gossip columns, cyber chatrooms and media types chatting over their cappuccinos for several months. Until Hawkins had slayed the demons, but not before cashing in on the process with a prime-time appearance on a confessional chat show and a fifteen-page spread in the city's leading celebrity glossy mag.

Hawkins' daughter spent much of her waking hours at the Little Angels Crèche, where the offspring of the moneyed began their gilded journey in life. Hawkins' black Mercedes SLK slipped quietly through the electronic gates at the rear of the building.

On hearing that some of the city's great and good deposited collected their children there on a regular basis, several of the lower echelons of the paparazzi had camped out at the front of the building. This irritation was soon dealt with: the rear access was offered to the parents so they could sidle in and out without any irritation from the noisome parasites.

The paparazzi had ended their temporary occupation indefinitely when one of their number had been abducted and had both of his hands smashed with a mallet. His mistake had been to snap a certain young child on her way out of the nursery, one Tess Bain. His erstwhile colleague had also received a similar warning as he was held upside down from the fourteenth floor of a multi-storey car park. Suffice to say, he sought new and less volatile prey after this.

Escorted by a young nursery nurse, Scarlet skipped out of the nursery clutching her Louis Vuitton satchel.

"Hi Mummy, we made pancakes," she said as she jumped into the leather upholstered passenger seat. Hawkins strapped her into the rear-facing car seat and they made off, Scarlet waving to her factotum as they went.

Hawkins was glad she had dropped a Valium before picking up her daughter. She was able to let the volley of childish babble wash over her, responding only with "Oh, lovely darling," and "Oh, really?"

She would grab a vodka and tonic when she got back and then have a couple of hours sleep. Thankfully, Latika, her Vietnamese live-in-nanny, would be on hand to deflect Scarlet's attention and cater to her every whim. These were her thoughts as she slowed the car and pointed it at the gates, awaiting the infra-red sensor to recognise the microchip planted in her car bonnet, which would swing the gates open. Security like this came at a cost, but peace of mind was priceless, or so the guy from the estate agents had told her when she had taken the lease out on the exclusive apartment in the gated community. The gates duly swung open and the sleek sports car nosed its way in.

"Aw shit," said Hawkins – a cleaner's cart was blocking the entrance to the underground parking garage. "Stay here a minute, darling; Mummy's going to have to move the stupid thing." Scarlet responded with a tide of babble which did not penetrate Hawkins's Valium haze, and she chose to ignore it, shutting the driver's door. Hawkins tottered across to the garage entrance on her Jimmy Choos and gave the cleaner's cart a shove – but it wouldn't budge.

Meanwhile, something caught Scarlet's attention – a ball launched from the bushes which populated the border of the complex. On the architect's impressions, the bushes were thinly spread out and the topiary border broke up the monotony of the fence line, but they were a security analyst's nightmare.

Hawkins renewed her efforts at moving the cleaner's cart, eventually realising that the brake was deployed on the rear wheels. She moved to knock it off with her foot; her heel caught and got trapped. She tried to pull it out but ended up going sprawling, in a flurry of tanned legs and expensive Agent Provocateur underwear, so hilarious that any pap would have sold his soul to get the shot. "Aw, you fucking bastard!" screeched Hawkins.

Transfixed by the ball and unaware of her mother's predicament, Scarlet had undone her safety belt, opened the car door and followed the ball into the thick foliage created by the interlocking Leylandii bushes. Her trajectory was interrupted when a pair of strong hands grabbed her and a hood was placed over her head. Hawkins had by this time righted herself, leaning precariously on the cleaner's cart.

The next thing she knew, a man in overalls and a Saddam Hussein mask had opened the door of the SLK and began reversing it towards the gates, which were opening, to let in a small white van whose sliding side door was already opened. Another Saddam Hussein was behind the wheel. Gripped by a surge of adrenaline and rage, Hawkins sprinted across and tried to wrench open the driver's door of her car as it moved off. The window opened and she was hit in the face with a liquid. Instantly her vision clouded and her mouth and nose clogged with mucus as the spray took effect. She collapsed to the floor screaming as the car pulled off.

"You bastards! My car, my beautiful face!" she screamed.

Across the road a number of flashes erupted from the front of a nondescript van. Dave Tuft clicked the switch with his thumb a few more times and then decided he really ought to help Melbourne's favourite newscaster to her feet. Well, maybe he'd call the office first; they wouldn't bloody believe it. He punched the speed dial on his phone, using his thumb, the only digit on both hands which was not swathed in a cast and undergoing extensive restorative surgery.

# Chandler Hospital, Northern Territory.

Walker awoke to see a burly uniformed cop standing over his hospital bed. His nose itched and he went to scratch it, but his effort was arrested by the steel bracelet around his wrist whose partner was clasped around the bed frame. "Take it easy, chap, you're not going anywhere fast," said the cop in a friendly voice.

"What the fuck happened to me?" asked Walker.

"Well, now you're firing on all cylinders again, that's exactly what we want you to tell us," said the cop.

# Central Melbourne.

Fiona Hawkins sat at the glass topped table of her kitchen and looked at the items on it. All were symbolic of the whirlwind of shit that she had found herself in just over two hours ago. The first was a large or at least the remnants of a large bloody Mary, easy on the tomato juice. The second, a leather folder containing her cheque book. The third was a nondescript pay-as-you-go mobile phone, the kind that was yours for $20 in any electronics store.

The story unfolded something like this.

Your daughter is kidnapped, you are maced, an apparently good Samaritan helps you back to your apartment, makes you a bloody Mary and then when you've just about got your vision back, calmly asks for $10,000 dollars to keep the embarrassing fall pictures and the kidnap out of the city's yellow or otherwise press. He settles for five in the form of a cheque and leaves.

A few minutes after he leaves an unidentified motorcycle courier leaves a Jiffy bag at the foot of the stairs to your apartment. Inside, the mobile phone and three Polaroid pictures of your daughter – unharmed.

The phone rang. Hawkins trembled, reached for the phone with one hand, and the glass of booze with the other. She said nothing, listened carefully, set her alarm clock and collapsed on the bed after another slug of vodka, and another Valium.

# Chandler Police Station, Northern Territory.

On paper, Jez Walker ticked all the boxes that the parameters of The Dingo profile had set when drawn up by Sandersen and the other experts on the Operation Nemesis team.

The *prima facie* evidence against him found at the scene and in the car looked good. These initial findings had been further bolstered by the team of detectives who had systematically searched his home on a hastily obtained search warrant. His PC had been seized and forensic IT officers, or hackers who helped the cops, were searching it meticulously. He had been arrested on the charge of failing to report a death so they could hold him for forty-eight hours while the hackers and the DNA lab did their work. This way the NT Police did not have to disclose or run the risk of disclosure that a suspect in The Dingo Case had been brought in. It gave them a convenient two days to question their suspect without potential for the proverbial egg on their faces. From a more altruistic perspective it also protected Walker from the media spotlight and the risk of being branded with the killer tag.

For all the green lights, though, there was still a whole bag of doubts around this apparent prime candidate for the murders. Sandersen was reaching extensively into this bag as she sat in the room adjacent to where Walker was being held. Seated at a Formica table and clad in a paper suit, his clothes having been taken for forensic analysis, Walker looked slightly dazed but still retained a high degree of composure. This apparent calmness meant only two things to Sandersen – either he was that special kind of psychopath who could compartmentalise their life easily and play two kinds of people, the family man and the killer – the classic Jekyll and Hyde scenario. Or he was simply innocent. The trouble for Sandersen was that the pictures seemed to overlap and contradict each other.

On one hand Walker had been in the locality of all the killings when they occurred, a fact corroborated not only by his meticulously kept diary, but also from his company's head office. All of the firm's cars were fitted with GPS tracking devices, which were used to organise employees' routes for appointments, act as a locator in case of auto theft and also as a means of surreptitiously ensuring that employees were going where they said they were going. Admittedly, Walker had no concrete alibis, but, as he had retorted, he hadn't known he would need one. This in itself was a no-win situation for both sides.

The only time he'd gotten needled was when Detective Peat had questioned about the manuscript of his book. Peat had probed him about some of the graphically sexual content, suggesting that Walker might want to re-enact some of his on-page antics off the page and into a carnal reality. Peat had thought he'd hit the mother-lode on pursuing this tack, but Sandersen had straightened him out on this one quickly enough. In her opinion these were merely the utterings of a married man dissatisfied with his sexual lot, who, in Walker's case, had given voice to them by putting them on the page.

Walker wasn't coming up on Sandersen's radar as a prime suspect. But for now, she'd wait for the test results.

She stretched and yawned. Her mind was clogged; her body ached from exhaustion and from a yearning for James. Before, she'd always kept business and pleasure separate, but this time it was different. Progress was being made. For once she couldn't devote all of her mind and being to the case. She'd come to the NT looking for a killer and instead found love with a man she'd least expected it from.

# Tullamarine Airport, Melbourne.

Arumpled and unshaven Adrian Marsh arrived at Tullamarine Airport on a scheduled flight from Darwin via a transfer at Brisbane. The documents were still taped to his chest as the unmarked Victoria Police Ford Falcon dropped him at the spacious suburban house which had become James' home from home.

James was standing at the door wearing jeans and a t-shirt, the only indicator of past issues being the shoulder holster he wore carrying a Glock 17. Behind him in a pancake holster, a .38 revolver. The detective who had driven the car flipped the boot open and grabbed Marsh's Livingstone travel bag from its cavernous interior.

"One very important person, delivered intact," smiled the detective.

"Thanks, Officer, very important prick, more like," replied James, a sarcastic smile crossing his face.

"With friends like you, who needs enemies?" retorted Marsh.

"It's a good job you drove him here: I hear Mr Marsh has problems staying on the road," smirked James, stepping down and embracing Marsh.

"Geez, you've put some weight on, you fat bastard," said James, patting Marsh's stomach.

"That's not beer gut, that's pure gold," said Marsh, patting the bundle of papers inside his shirt. "Let me get inside and get my shirt off and I'll show you."

"Well there's an offer I can't refuse!" said James, truculently.

"Detective, you better get off. There's things gonna happen here that'll make your hair curl," joked Marsh.

The young detective smiled back, got in the driver's seat and swung the car off the drive and down the suburban street.

"Righty-oh, you go and get a shit, shower and shave, and you can give me an update," said James.

"Sure thing – I'll be with you in half an hour," said Marsh, disappearing into the house.

Fresh from his ablutions, Marsh came through to the kitchen, poured himself a coffee, loaded up a bagel with scrambled eggs and made his way through to the huge open space which had been given the inadequate title of living room. James was sprawled across a chaise longue from a designer boutique in the city which probably cost six months of his salary at least. An empty coffee mug sat next to him. He put the typed report down on the coffee table and looked up.

"You've been a busy boy," said James.

"Sure thing, while you've been hogging the limelight I've been at the coalface."

Ever the journalist, Marsh had put the collated findings of his efforts into a concise report which James had spent the previous twenty minutes reading.

"So, let me tell you what I've garnered from this and you fill me in on anything I get wrong," said James.

"Sure, go ahead," said Marsh, through a mouthful of bagel.

"Okay, it's mid-nineties and the whole NT is riven through with this Brotherhood organisation; a sort of Masons without the funny handshakes. Everything from school buildings to highways is cut and dried, brown envelopes aplenty for everyone. Down at the bottom of the pile, the low rank cops also take kickbacks for looking the other way on drink-driving and if any of The Brotherhood's sprogs get caught with weed or junk, they get a ride home in an unmarked and nothing goes down on paper."

"So into the middle of this comes The Dingo – he kills a bunch of women. Unsurprisingly, it creates a fair bit of fuss that attracts unwanted attention, and even The Brotherhood can't buy up everyone, despite their best efforts to muzzle the newshounds like you," said James, distractedly swirling the remains of his coffee.

"So it's in everyone's interest to get The Dingo off the scene. Along comes Calvin Miller and does a great job by shooting some cops and getting eviscerated in the process. The trail goes cold and everyone's happy... until this latest set of murders, which brings us to this missing police report, or should I say, thanks to you – mislaid police report," said James making for the well-stocked drinks cabinet and fixing himself a vodka and orange, plinking in a handful of ice-cubes from a hand-carved ice bucket.

"That's right. There was plenty of dirty stuff going on for the best part of a decade," said Marsh. "I pulled a few strings and got access to the Black Archive. This is the proverbial Pandora's box which was a record of actual police reports, etc, that had enough to put all the members of The Brotherhood behind bars for a stretch or at the very least publicly disgrace them," said Marsh.

"So while it existed everyone had the Sword of Damocles hanging over them, preventing anyone from whistle-blowing or squealing," said James.

"Exactly. Everyone had a vested interest in keeping their traps shut," said Marsh.

"And the gatekeepers of the Black Archive were the cops themselves," added James.

"That's right. Pass me a beer, would you," said Marsh.

"Except some cops had made a few copies to ensure they had a fail-safe mechanism, if the whole can of worms ever got opened, including our good friend Ferguson," said James, ripping the top off a Carlton Cold and passing it to Marsh.

"Yes, it seems that the whole thing got resurrected again after Caulfield took up the Commissioner's job. His predecessor, Elliot Murray, was one of the key proponents of The Brotherhood. He left with a clean sheet but there were plenty of rumours trailing in his wake," said Marsh, taking a swig of his beer. "And Caulfield stirred the hornet's nest when he asked for the archives to be moved to Timber Creek for Operation Nemesis. A few people got the heebie-jeebies about what could be found out, if people looked in the right places. It seems that about fifty cartons of documents never made it there. Murray had a few fellow travellers with a vested interest in keeping things under wraps for a whole lot longer," he added.

"So why all the fuss about this one car stopped on one night and how did you get onto it?" asked James.

"Well, it was the mere fact that too many people seemed to want to keep it from me that raised this old newshound's hackles," said Marsh. "Secondly, we owe a debt of gratitude to your friend from Poland, Ms Vukasin. Apparently, she studied graphology as part of her degree, in order to help her analyse documents from the KGB archive where she worked as an intern for a summer, investigating deaths of political opponents to the Soviet-backed regime in Poland.

"Well, she analysed the victims' handwriting on confessions comparing it with that of their normal handwriting as a way of seeing if the victims' confessions had been given under duress. I had my suspicions about a couple of the documents in the last Dingo files so I asked her to take a look," said Marsh.

"Phew," said James whistling through his teeth, "a mean shot *and* a graphologist, she's wasted mending stock fences."

"Quite," said Marsh, obviously aching to reach the crux of his story. "So, she analysed a couple of the dodgy-looking police files. In her opinion, the one from the night in question was a forgery and the ink on it was much more recent," said Marsh.

"So that set you on the trail of Sutton and Ferguson," said James.

"Yep, they were old muckers of mine anyway, I used to buy them a beer plus change for the odd snippet of information. I didn't realise they were on the take both ways though, the lousy finks," he added.

# Balmoral Hotel, Chandler, Northern Territory.

An accomplice? Was there mileage for this? The enigma at the centre of the case. If so, it would in one instance solve several of the inconsistencies at the centre of the investigation, but in the same instance derail and overturn a majority of all the work carried out so far. Not only that but it would also mean treading over old ground, requiring all previous lines of investigation to be re-examined now the parameters had been redrawn. If this theory were to be presented it would inevitably cause ructions. These were the thoughts occupying Sandersen's mind as she sank deeper into the bathtub, chock full of aromatherapy oils. She submerged herself once more and rose from the water to reach for a glass of chilled Chardonnay. Next to the thin-stemmed wine glass lay a nickel-plated .38 revolver, a gift from Marsh who had dropped in to see here on his way to Melbourne.

She took a sip of the wine and emerged from the tub, towelled off and put on a fluffy hotel bathrobe. Before she kicked the hornet's nest she needed to expound her theory to someone. She picked up the telephone and dialled. Several thousand miles away, a telephone rang in Melbourne.

# Supermax, HM Prison, Barwon, Victoria.

Cyrus Bain had been taken off suicide watch, but was still kept in isolation, ostensibly for his own protection, but he knew that it was to keep him out of touch with the general prison population. The mobile phone had reconnected him with the world again and his confidence and cunning had returned with relish, like spring days stretching out their limbs in the light after the dark dull days of winter. The observation hatch in his cell door opened and a face appeared.

"Bain, get your pants on, you've got an appointment with that pretty woman again. Christ, you get more pussy visiting you in here than I can get on the outside. I'm beginning to think I made the wrong choice of career," said the guard with a hint of earnestness, something which did not go unnoticed by Bain.

He was cuffed and marched to a waiting Department of Corrections van and driven to the studios of Oceania TV. Hawkins had insisted that the technical requirements of the modern TV couldn't be met in a prison cell. "She'd need a fucking truck just for her make-up," one wag in the studio had joked to an appreciative audience.

While security was nothing like that during the trial, Bain was still guarded by three prison guards, and two uniform cops were patrolling the vicinity of the studios.

Bain was hustled into a room with a high ceiling and two facing couches. It had been agreed that he would have his handcuffs removed during the interview. "How's he supposed to wring his hands full of remorse for his misspent time, if his hands are shackled together?" Usha Salina, the producer, had said.

Salina was a devout Muslim and wore a full burka, contrasting sharply with Fiona Hawkins who had dressed up to the nines in order "to make Bain jizz in his pants", a confidence she had shared with her make-up artist. Bain did not escape the TV makeover, having foundation and powder applied. A few minutes later, the minions scuttled away, the studio lights went up and the cameras rolled. Bain was looking his best for his fifteen minutes of fame.

# Safehouse, Melbourne.

Adrian Marsh had been hammering the phone, racking up a huge bill, no doubt. He had spent the preceding day ensconced in the snug-cum-study of the big house which was James' suburban hideout.

Taking Ferguson's advice, he had chased up dealers of American muscle cars, spoken to shipping companies and importers. The internet had been invaluable too. Finally, he hit pay dirt. He had traced a Pontiac Firebird which had come into Australia via Melbourne. Its previous owner had been in the UK near Birmingham. After waiting several tense hours, the phone rang. Marsh jolted awake. He had been slumped in the leather office chair, the flotsam and jetsam of a paperchase and a cold mug of coffee on the desk lit by an angle-poise lamp. He riffled through the pile of papers and picked up the phone. It was John Burnham, a private investigator and former colleague of Marsh's.

"Hey, Marshie. I think we hit the mother-lode," said the raspy smoker's voice.

"Why's that?" asked Marsh snappily.

"Well, thanks for the praise there, mate, just shoot the messenger, why don't you?"

"Sorry, John, it's been a long day. What's the news?"

"Well I traced the ownership through DVLA at Swansea. The name was bullshit. But the address was kosher!" said Burnham.

"Someone trying to cover their tracks?" wondered Marsh.

"Exactly. Anyway, I checked the address out. The new house owner didn't have a clue, but the old busybody over the road gave me the whole nine yards. The car owner was a guy in his forties, lived alone. Didn't really speak to him much, just to say 'Hello'.

But then one day he turns up with a young girl. Says she's his niece, but the old biddy swears it's his daughter. So one Sunday he's out polishing his car and the old dame, who's a Catholic, is walking off to church. She said to the guy, 'Oh would your daughter like to come with me to church.' Well, he went apeshit! And told her he'd had enough of priests for a lifetime."

"I can empathise with that," said Marsh.

"I think it was worse than an arse spanking by the Christian Brothers," replied Burnham.

"Abuse?"

"Possibly and that's what brings me to Patricia Moore and her little crusade," said Burnham.

Marsh's tiredness disappeared and a surge of adrenaline hit him as he grabbed a pen and gripped the telephone receiver a little tighter.

# Police Headquarters, Melbourne.

The Chief Commissioner's personal line rang, raising him from his reverie. He'd been pondering how, now the case had come to an end, he'd take his long-suffering wife and kids on holiday to Florida.

He'd even had his PA get him a bunch of brochures when she went out on her lunch break. There was no introduction, just a startled voice he recognised as one of his senior officers. "You won't fucking believe this, Cyrus Bain has escaped from custody. And we can't contact Lawrence James."

The Chief Commissioner slammed down the phone, swept the holiday brochures into the bin and stomped angrily to the conference room.

\*\*\*

You'd thought he was creepy when he'd been following you, but now you realised that he'd just been so concerned about finally connecting with you.

You'd met him at Wimpy behind the bowling alley – convenient but discreet. He'd gone to hug you but instinctively you'd shrunk back. You'd explain a few meetings later. You'd shared a laugh about the way he had followed you and how you threatened him with the knife. "Killer eyes" he said you'd got – how prescient that was in hindsight.

The excuse of going to Jennie's had begun to wear thin, so you invented Darren, your new boyfriend. He lived down the other side of town. "Just don't go and get knocked up, I don't want you dropping a sprog before you're out of school uniform." Those were your mum's words of wisdom on learning the news.

You realised later that he wanted to protect you from the less than blissful events surrounding your birth, but he didn't realise at the time that your young adult life had been much more than a living hell until he'd found you. On the fourth meeting – a visit to a nature reserve under the weeping willows, amongst the happy families feeding the swans, ducks and geese – it had all come spilling out. You'd arrived wearing a bandage on your forearm and told him the truth – Kelly Watson had poured a pan of water over your arm, saying a frigid bitch like you should stop looking at her boyfriend. It had hurt like hell. You hadn't slept for three nights because of the pain.

He listened intently to you, but then something changed and he seemed to bristle like a fox that has heard the scream of a rabbit in distress. He'd asked what you were going to do about it. "Nothing," you'd replied, saying how if you fought back it would only come back at you worse later.

"That was then, this is now. Now you've got me," he said supportively. "I want you to show me where this Kelly Watson lives," he'd said.

That was how you'd spent the afternoon sitting outside Kelly Watson's middle-class, detached house. He'd dropped you off and told you to meet him next morning. You'd got up and made for school. Half way there you'd cut down the alley between the allotments by the canal known as Cat Gallows. His car was parked on the piece of wasteland next to the allotments and a garage door was propped open with a brick. You'd gone into the darkened interior, the smell of creosote, engine oil and fear hit you.

"Shut the door and lock it," his voice said. You did as you were told. The light from a single light bulb snapped on and the room was illuminated. He was wearing a one-piece boiler suit and a surgical mask. You were not alone. A figure whimpered and sniffed in the middle of the room. You recognised the clothing; it was the same school uniform that you were wearing. He pulled the hessian sack off her head. It was Kelly Watson, tied and gagged to a wooden chair. "I'm going to ask you nicely to apologise," he said. He pulled the gag down. "Fuck off, paedo!" she spat, apparently unconcerned by her predicament.

The hand shot out from nowhere and slapped her across the face. Before she could recover from the shock, he backhanded even harder, a palpable slap emanated through the room. Her eyes ballooned in terror.

Barely out of breath he'd asked. "Perhaps you'll reconsider now?"

"Fuck off, you paedo," she'd spat back.

That was enough for you – you ran forward and punched her as hard as you could. She squealed in pain. But you'd hurt your fist.

"No, darling. You'll hurt yourself doing that. Use the hard part of your hand, along the side, like this."

He belted her once more. "And then come back like this." He smashed his hand back across her face. You had another go as he looked on. This time you hit her much harder without hurting your hand.

Blood trickled from her mouth. "We'd always thought you were a fucking weirdo and thought Martin wasn't your dad. It's cos your mum's a slag and can't keep her legs closed that you don't know who your dad is… sla–" Her words were cut off with a killer left hook. Her mouth burst open and she gagged, choked and spat out three teeth. She'd slumped forward, crying and sobbing.

Then he'd picked up the rounder's bat and given it to you. You knew what you had to do. You had crossed the Rubicon and there was no going back. Just like Caesar, you learnt about in history. You felt the weight of the bat in your hand – it felt good. You swung it at her, hitting her in the chest and she groaned. Then a thought hit you: why let her go quickly? You smashed the bat into her kneecap and were rewarded with a cracking sound and a scream of pain. You weren't quite sure how many blows it took for her to die, but you knew it felt good. Eventually, her laboured breathing gave way to a gurgle, and then a rattle and she died.

He stuck a syringe in her arm and pushed the plunger down, wiped the syringe and threw it on the dirty floor.

"Okay, love, let's go, just got to tidy up," he said. He pulled a blow lamp and a can of petrol. He lit the blow lamp and you left.

As you drove off, the garage exploded in a ball of flame. Over a burger at Wimpy he asked you, "So did you enjoy it?"

You told the truth. "Yes, it was good," you said, pausing to take a slurp of milkshake.

"The next one will be more fun, but we'll have to be tidier," he said, sipping his black coffee.

"When?" you ask.

"Soon enough. Don't worry, you'll get your chance to say goodbye," he said.

The news came out three days later; your mum was reading the paper as she smoked a cigarette at the kitchen table. "See one of your little friends was a smackhead, blew herself up down by Cat Gallows," she said. "I hope you haven't been down there?" she asked, thumping the newspaper.

You went upstairs with a smile on your face. You remember the weight of the wooden bat in your hand and how good it felt. Then you did your homework.

The best was to come a week later – it was a fantasy beyond your wildest dreams. He'd arranged it all for you. And the sweet feeling of killing had returned. Again the revenge would be served cold and the set-up perfect.

# Safehouse, Melbourne.

James had offered to drive Marsh to Tullamarine for his flight to the UK and had relished the chance to get behind the wheel of a car after weeks of being cooped up in hotel suites or hustled from cop car to cop car in an armoured convoy like the paranoid dictator of some banana republic. He wouldn't be entering the terminal, swathed as he was in firearms and a Kevlar vest. Bain might be behind bars, but there were plenty enough of his henchmen around still happy to cash in on the bounty which, according to informants, still stood, despite Bain's conviction. Much as he loathed saying it, James found the city restrictive and his return reminded him of why he'd been so eager to go to the NT.

He missed the open spaces where you could see your opponents coming for you, and, most of all, he missed Sandersen.

Seeing James was preoccupied, Marsh kept his conversation to the minimum, his mind also occupied on how the secrets of a killer, whose habitat was the heat and dust of the Northern Territory, possibly lay in the rain-sodden, overcrowded islands that were the UK.

# Central Melbourne.

Scarlet had been returned to Fiona Hawkins exactly one hour after she had signed her witness statement at police headquarters.

She had told them she had no knowledge of Bain's escape plan.

During the first break, Bain had been taken from the studio to the bathrooms. A guard had stood outside the door until the moment the fire alarm had gone off.

He'd been beckoned to the end of the corridor by an anxious stage manager trying to account for the whereabouts of all the people in the studio. Distracted for no more than thirty or forty seconds, he'd returned to stand guard outside the door.

Nothing had happened, save for Hawkins's producer, Usha, appearing from the women's bathroom.

He'd eventually gone into the men's bathroom, baton drawn, to find no one in there, just a pile of clothes. A female police officer had entered the women's bathroom and found Usha out cold on the floor, clad only in underwear, but covered by a blanket. She'd been grabbed from behind and had a cloth placed over her face that had made her black out. Chloroform, old school but effective in knowledgeable hands. A city-wide APB had gone out for Bain. Hawkins was just glad to get her kid back, not from any filial love, but from the chance the kidnapping might have made the headlines.

Lawrence James was blissfully unaware of this as he nosed the car through the electric gates of the suburban poolside paradise.

His phone had been turned off since someone had leaked his mobile number to the press. He got out of the car and stretched.

Then he realised something was wrong. He dropped to the floor, did a commando roll and came up holding his Glock 17. He looked straight into the eyes of Cyrus Bain, and the ominous looking barrel of a Desert Eagle handgun held steadily in his left hand.

"Checkmate," chuckled Bain as he sat in a poolside chair. "Let's put the guns down and have a beer, eh?" he said with an expansive wave of his hand. James knew Bain would have the odds in his favour: he was a calculating operator.

James' heart was pounding as the adrenaline surged through his body and the sweat poured down his back as he calculated the odds. He decided to play ball.

"Okay, it's pretty surreal but I'll join you," said James. He pulled the magazine out of the gun and held it up so Bain could see it clearly. He put both on the ground in front of him, and took a step back, his arms hanging at his side.

"Good call," said Bain, who did the same and put the magazine and the handgun on the sun lounger to his side.

He leant down into the pool and fished a six pack of beers from a net suspended in the pool. Suddenly, there was movement from both left and right of James. From behind the pool-house stepped Robbie holding a sawn-off shotgun. From behind the car came Irish, holding a Mach 10 sub-machine gun.

James breathed easier; he'd made the right decision. He was still wearing a Kevlar vest under his shirt. It would stop shotgun pellets, but slugs from a Mach 10 would go through it like a fork through crispy duck. Irish moved forward and put down James' revolver, still in the pancake holster on the sun lounger.

"My, we are a boy scout, aren't we," said Bain.

"Well, when you're up against a professional you've got to be prepared," said James.

Bain ripped the caps off two beers and James took one, taking a hefty gulp and sat down a metre or so away from Bain. Robbie had picked up James' gun and put it on the table.

"Enough guns to arm a banana republic there," said Robbie.

"Guns might be your style, Robbie, but I prefer doing things with a little more subtlety," said Bain.

"Like bombs on planes?" asked James pointedly.

Irish shifted uneasily and twisted the earpiece he wore. "Boss, we're gonna have company soon, probably got ten minutes to get clear," he said, in his Northern Irish brogue.

"So, to my reason for coming here," said Bain, wiping beer foam from his top lip.

"Spill it," said James.

"Well, as you know, some of your more financially astute colleagues took the opportunity to work for me. I thought I'd offer you the same opportunity, especially as you're the Chief Commissioner's golden boy. No one would be able to touch you."

"They're a bunch of amoral scab necks and you're a murdering scumbag, pardon my French," spat James contemptuously.

"Whoa, easy, tiger, you're a bit feisty today," said Bain. Robbie bristled and swung the shotgun.

"Easy there too, Robbie," said Bain with a wave of his hand. "I wasn't always a murdering scumbag."

"So what happened to you? Your daddy miss some of your school sports days and turned you into a psycho, that it?" asked James, looking for a chink in his armour. The barb turned without inflicting a scratch. "I'm sure my colleague, Dr Sandersen, would love to hear it, but I think you're an animal that belongs in a cage," said James.

"I'm not a psycho, just a businessman," said Bain.

"Sandersen might like you as a specimen to study like a spider in a jar, I suppose," mused James.

Bain's eyes narrowed but he composed himself imperceptibly.

"Is that what she's doing with you, is it? Are you her little project, her little wounded soldier boy?" retorted Bain. "She's been getting the likes of me off the hook for years. Gangster, sure, but my dad beat me when I wet the bed, boo-hoo, boo-hoo, give me a suspended sentence."

"She's the best at her job I've ever seen, she's going to help me bag The Dingo and when we've finished we'll come after you," snarled James.

"She might be poacher turned gamekeeper now, but only after taking the gold from most of the city's crims… I mean businessmen. We can all be fucking moral when we're driving an SLK to Woomera Heights," said Bain.

"Tell me your story. then. I suppose you started out stealing sweets and graduated to stealing lives?" said James.

"Stealing lives?" asked Bain.

"Sure, you sell your junk and screw people's lives. They end up selling their ass or their pussy for a few bucks to get their fix or kids end up selling the copper fittings from their folks' bathrooms."

"Fuck them – it's a free world – their choice," said Bain.

"You better tell me your story: it'll make a nice little bedtime story for Sandersen," said James.

"A good fuck, is she?" asked Bain.

"As a matter of fact, she is," said James. "Better than bending for the soap like you'll be doing for the next thirty years. You'll need the little purple pill by the time you get out."

"I'll tell you my story as a testament to the fact that you're going to leave this predicament alive and the fact that I'll stop Robbie blowing your knee caps off," said Bain, matter-of-factly. Robbie chuckled.

"Seeing as you're being so magnanimous, I'll listen to it," said James. "But I'll need another beer to get me through."

Bain leant down and fished out another beer, ripped off the top and passed it to James, who nodded his thanks.

"We were seventeen, me and my best friend, Dave Jones – we'd just passed our carpentry exams. The town I lived in was a one-street piece of shit, so we'd boost a car and get over to Laramie, the nearest town. It was a piece of shit too, but it had a grog shop that didn't ask for ID.

"So this particular night I told my folks I was going out for some smokes and went out. About six minutes later I found a ute with the keys kept behind the sunshield, so I thought I'd take it for a spin. I rolled a joint from my big bag of grass, popped the top on a can of booze and was soon burning along for all I was worth, about eighty k in that jalopy. Anyways, all of a sudden a great bastard of a wombat decides to scratch his arse in the middle of the road. I hit the bastard at full tilt and creamed him, but he was such a big fucker that he buckled the wheel and I went off the road into a drainage ditch.

"Now, normally, I'd have cut loose and left the ute for Johnny Anybody to come and sort out. But this ute belonged to Baz Pinner, a right hard man, he used to prop up the local bar and was always bragging about how he'd give his missus a shiner on a regular basis. A real man, he supposed. Anyways, I knew he'd tear me limb from limb if he found out and I'd be a dead man."

Bain paused, taking a swig from his beer. Irish and Robbie looked intrigued, their grip on their weapons relaxing somewhat, but James wasn't about to gamble with his life.

"So I had to do something sharpish – so I hoofed it to a house nearby. There was no way I was going to knock on the door and ask Mrs Miggins or whoever if I could use their phone. I was steaming and stoned and I had wombat guts all over my jeans. So I went round the back and forced the door with a piece of steel I carried. I got in, found the phone in the kitchen and belled my mate Dave. His dad had a Land Rover, something big enough to pull the ute out of the ditch and get us back in one piece. So I told him to get his arse out there sharpish with a tow-rope. So he agreed. I helped myself to a couple of tinnies and a cake from their fridge. I made myself comfortable down the road a little ways from the ute in case any plods decided to have a sticky-beak and rolled myself a fat one.

"About fifteen minutes later he turns up in this Land Rover that looks like it's something out of Mad Max, covered in stickers and big exhausts - all that clobber. Best of all, he's got a winch on the back. So after he's bawled me out for getting him off the sofa where he'd been watching Aussie rules, he gets the winch on and tells me to get in the ute and see if I can reverse it out. So I jumped in and fired her up – she starts up and I bang her in reverse. I give her too much gas and go shooting back. Whump! I slam on the anchors and get out.

"He's lying under the back wheels, his legs crushed and he's bleeding from the head. He can't see me and there's blood in his eyes. He's rasping and I know he'll peg it, so I make for the hills. I took off in the Land Rover, and three days later I was here in Melbourne. I know I was a prize cunt for doing what I did to Dave, but I knew then what I know now – it's a matter of the survival of the fittest. He was unlucky. I hit the grog and stayed on the bottle for two years after that. Then I worked at a breaker's yard winding clocks back and making good," Bain said, his sordid tale concluded.

"And Dave, what happened to him?" asked James.

"They scraped him into an ambulance and took him to hospital. He lingered on for a few weeks and then died from pneumonia he contracted in hospital," said Bain woefully.

"Well, you started as you meant to go on, I suppose," said James.

"I wanted to join the army as soon as I turned eighteen. When I told my dad he beat seven shades of shit out of me. Screamed blue murder at me. He did two tours in 'Nam – long-range reconnaissance patrols. He had a bag full of dried Viet Cong ears in the garage. My mum said he'd been off his fruit since the time he came back from his first tour. Life deals you a shitty hand and you deal with it," Bain said.

"Well, let me tell you a story, then," said James.

"Sure, but you can tell me in the car after Robbie's put a blindfold on you," said Bain, taking a last swallow of his beer and putting the empty can on the sun lounger with the guns.

James stood up and Robbie slipped a sleeping mask, like the ones given out on long haul flights, over James' eyes. Strong arms bundled him into what was, judging by the step up, a four-wheel drive. Irish sat next to him, the barrel of a weapon nudged into his ribs. Robbie gunned the vehicle's powerful engine and sped off towards the outskirts of the city.

James' thoughts began to stray to a bullet in the nape of the neck as he kneeled on the blacktop of a lonely Victorian highway, when Bain's voice interjected.

"So, you were gonna tell me a story?"

"Well, if you're all sitting comfortably then I'll begin," said James.

"Fucking old school," said Robbie, surprised at the reference to an old British radio programme for kids, well before the confessional style Oprah Winfrey or the bear pits of the Jerry Springer show.

"That's as old as the hills, me and me mam used to listen to that while I had my tea," interjected Irish.

"Well, this walk down memory lane's all well and good for you bloody poms, but it means jack shit to me," snapped Bain. "Now cut to the chase or I'll shoot my fucking self in the face out of sheer bloody boredom."

"Okay, here goes," said James. He shuffled in his seat. Irish kept the gun jammed tight on him, ever the professional gunman, but James could sense an easing of tension in the vehicle as the men's attention focussed on him. He felt the car leave the city's highways as they entered a steep curving bend which at this time and distance from the city could mean only one place. A beautiful, but lonely place. But James had been in lonely places before and survived. He fully intended to survive this. A jab in the guts with a gun jerked him back to the present.

"Come on, copper, tell us your story," urged Irish, earnestly.

"I'm an only child, right – I grew up in a little town, which was mostly rural. I had no brothers and sisters, so I got used to making friends fast and keeping them. My best friend was Danny."

James paused to lick his lips and bring more saliva into his mouth. He felt a spot of moisture hit his face and thought for a second one of them had spat on him. He quickly realised it wasn't their style, plus if they had done it there'd have been a darn sight

P. J. Nash

more phlegm. There was a whir as Robbie rolled up the electric windows. It was raining outside.

"Danny used to bunk off from school a lot and spent his days messing around the fields. He had an air rifle, so we spent most of the time shooting at birds, usually missing. Anyway, one day I met him after I'd done my homework – I was kept in by my mum for at least two hours to do extra study."

There was a squeal of tyres as the ABS kicked in, holding the four-wheel drive on the rain slicked road. Robbie gunned the engine again as they negotiated out of the hairpin bend.

James picked up where he had left off.

"So, me and Danny were hanging out one day and he said to me. 'Let's go up to the ridge', which was hilarious, as he couldn't pronounce his Rs so it came out like 'widge'. 'Where's the ridge?' I asked. He told me it was one of his favourite places – where he went to get away from his folks. His dad was a mean drunk and used to smack him around. We went up this low rise in the fields – where I'm from it's pretty flat, so this ridge was something special even though it was maybe only a hundred feet high. We got to the top, sweating, and Danny broke out some fags he had stolen from his dad. Danny went for a piss and disappeared.

"I was taking in the view and taking a drag on my tab when three guys appeared. One of them was Jarred Mahoney; a real sadistic prick who hated me, because he thought I was posh, as my parents owned their own house. And most of all, because I was Catholic and went to a different school."

"I know what that's like," agreed Irish.

"He didn't know what being Catholic meant, but he knew it made me different and that was good enough for him," said James, bitterly.

The car slowed again as it went through another S-bend, one of many on this particular stretch of road. It confirmed James' first suspicions as to where he was being taken, though he could not work out the purpose. Whatever it was, he wasn't going to get an ice cream and, if he was going for a swim, he wouldn't be needing his trunks or a towel. He swallowed, his mouth dry with fear and the hoppy taste of the beer from earlier.

"So this piece of shit, Jarred, and his pals saw me and decided to have some fun. They all laid into me and though I got a few punches in, I was soon down on the floor and blood was all over my face. 'What we gonna do with this cunt now?' Jarred asked his mates. 'I reckon we tie him up and make an example of him,' they said.

"So they tied me to a tree with some baler twine they found from somewhere. It hurt like hell. They give me a few more slaps and then the evil shit Jarred said, 'I'm gonna cut his cock off, then he won't be able to shag any of our women and turn them into Catholic sluts and have fifty fuckin' kids.' One of the guys pulled my trousers and pants down and Jarred pulled out an evil looking knife and started towards me.

"Then suddenly he fell over stone cold, into a heap and he bit his tongue as he went down, a slick of blood trickling out onto the grass. Danny was standing behind him clutching a cricket bat. He'd slugged him good and proper. There was a rustling in the bushes and two of Danny's brothers came out of the trees pushing the two other of my tormentors in front of them – they'd both got baseball bats. 'You've got a real wiener,' said Danny, staring at my cock. We both laughed. Danny and his brothers wanted to work over the other two guys, but I pleaded for them, saying they hadn't done much and were probably scared of Jarred as much as I was. They ran off. We left Jarred to his own devices. His parents found him later that evening. Danny's blow had fractured his skull, causing extensive brain damage. Nobody ever came forward about the attack.

"That's the moral of the story for me. You can rule by fear and intimidation for a while, but not for ever, because one day someone bigger and scarier's gonna come along. Or just whack you when you're not looking. I learnt to join the biggest gang that sticks together and has the most guns," smirked James.

"There endeth the lesson from Brother James," said Bain sarcastically, clapping his hands together in mock applause.

"It's just a shame some of your 'family' would be glad to see you dead after you ratted them out," he added.

"Well you can't love all your kith and kin now, can you?" retorted James. "And do you really think all your bosom buddies aren't gonna fight over the sweets while the big bad Bain has left the sweetie jar unattended?" asked James, attempting to needle Bain.

"They'll do as they're fucking well told," said Bain, obviously riled.

"Now, now, boys play nice," said Robbie, obviously relishing the pissing contest between Bain and James.

"Sorry to spoil the party atmosphere, but we're here, boss," cut in Irish.

The car slowed to a halt – both rear doors were opened and James was pushed out. His blindfold was pulled off and he blinked a few times as the sea breeze hit him. He was facing the beautiful rock stack formation known as The Twelve Apostles. The rocks were at the end of the 243-kilometre Great Ocean Road.

"Beautiful isn't it?" said Bain, drinking in the view. "Thought I'd come out here and take a last gander before I make myself scarce," he said ruefully.

Robbie performed a minutely precise three-point turn and the front passenger door opened. Bain jumped in, leant down into the footwell and came up again.

*This is fucking it*, thought James, waiting for the stab of pain that signalled the beginning of the end of his life.

"Catch, you dopey bastard," said Bain, lobbing a half-litre bottle of chilled water at James who stood, open mouthed in disbelief. "See you around, James – I got a plane to catch," shouted Bain, with a flourish of his hand.

Robbie gunned the engine, the wheels bit the cliff top gravel and the four-wheel drive sped away. James fell on the floor, a wave of nervous tension sweeping through him. He was transfixed by the living contradiction that was Bain, a man who, on the one hand sold drugs to kids and had people tortured and shot with impunity, yet would not leave a man – who helped send him to prison – on a lonely road without water.

He sat down on the edge of the cliffs cross-legged and stared at the setting sun, desperately desiring a cigarette.

An hour later a phone call was made to Geelong Police Station to report a burning vehicle at the entrance of an apparently disused airfield. The caller said that the car had burst into flames just minutes after a Lear Jet had taxied in, turned round and taken off again, all in a matter of a few minutes.

*\*\**

You came home from school, full of trepidation. This was the danger time, between the time you get home, and when Mum gets back from work. When Martin "pops back to get something".

You open the back door and see the lights are on in the hall and upstairs. Martin's trainers, big like a pair of clown shoes.

"Up here, Alison," he says.

It's him, not Martin.

You get the feeling of déjà vu – it's fear, you know how that feels, but this is different – it's someone else's fear. The door to the garage from the kitchen is open, held back by the kitchen bin. You go into the garage, empty now as Mum has taken the car to work. Then you see them.

Martin is standing on the bottom step of an aluminium stepladder.

He is standing on the floor next to him.

Slung from the hook where Martin's punch bag normally hangs is a linen rope. One end is tied around the heavy beam; the other formed into a noose around Martin's neck. He can't look you in the eye, merely casts his eyes to the floor.

Then you see the gun, black and sleek. A handgun: you recognise it from a movie you've seen, Pulp Fiction or Reservoir Dogs.

He jams it into Martin's neck, a finger on the trigger. "It's payback time, Martin," he says.

He beckons you over. "Do you want to do the honours?" he asks.

"I'd love to, it's just a shame we can't torture him first," you say.

"Don't worry, he'll suffer okay," he says.

He hands you the gun. The metal is cold and the weapon heavy. You feel the power of it. The power of life and death.

"Get up the steps, you bastard," you say, pushing the gun into the small of Martin's back.

He mounts the steps.

"Now jump!" you say, smashing the gun into his back.

You are not sure if Martin goes willingly or if it is an involuntary reaction, but he jumps into the air and his body spasms. His feet jerk and kick and his hands grasp the rope as he swings in the air. A gurgling emanates from his throat.

He moves the steps as Martin attempts to put his feet back on them. It takes fifteen minutes for him to die.

The note he has written and the external hard drive full of child pornography planted in his car ensure his life doesn't end in a dignified manner.

A week later you pack a suitcase, and leave for Australia on a fake passport.

# Near Birmingham, United Kingdom.

The rattle of the snack trolley jolted Adrian Marsh as it passed. The young woman hauling it down the train invited weary passengers to refresh themselves. Marsh raised his hand to grab the girl's attention as she had gone past him down the aisle. She returned with the trolley.

"Can I get a large black coffee, please?" he said, reaching for his wallet.

Thirty hours previously Marsh had boarded a plane in Melbourne. Now he was bowling along through the English countryside at a hundred miles an hour to reach his final destination, a small market town in the English Midlands where his investigations might throw some light on one Derek Havilland, a lecturer in sociology and one-time owner of a Pontiac Firebird whose presence on a certain piece of road at a certain time had been the inspiration for a major cover-up. He handed her a five pound note and she handed him his change; not as much as he had expected. Prices had gone up. He took a swig of the coffee, pricey but good. In the old days of British Rail, the coffee tasted like it had been made of acorns and the water drawn from a cesspit. Taking a deep swig of the scalding brew, Marsh yearned for a good cigar to complement the caffeine hit, but it would have to do its work single-handedly.

He sat back in his seat and mulled over how The Dingo Case had taken over his recent life and how it trailed back into the past to when he had been a young man, lean and fit, running 10ks every day with a healthy young daughter and a beautiful wife. He could just about comprehend the bitter loss of a child or loved one through a car crash or cancer. Both of these tragic events had marred his life. His daughter lost to leukaemia three years ago. And his wife had been hit head-on by a drunk driver, who was acquitted when the case came to court.

The cops had been friends of the driver's. By the time they had got him back to the station via a circuitous route and then hooked him up to a breathalyser, he was a hair's breadth below the legal limit. With hindsight, Marsh now saw the far-reaching hand of The Brotherhood encroaching into his own life. As he ran his mind over certain previously inexplicable events, they seemed to make sense in the light of this new perspective.

But The Brotherhood's motives were still driven by the age-old forces of greed and self-advancement. What he couldn't comprehend was the banal villainy of someone – or some people – who would intentionally seek to harm anyone for no logical reason. For him, the hunt for The Dingo had been a decade-long obsession, and in James and Sandersen he had found kindred spirits who shared his desire to catch the killer.

A sudden pang of guilt hit Marsh as the green blurred countryside rolled by. He thought of the wasted evenings and days he'd spent in his study, assembling clippings, and in archives; and dark nights and early mornings spent in car parks and seedy bars meeting contacts that might be able to offer him a snippet of information, however spurious. Time he could have spent with his wife and daughter – time he would never get back. He uttered a quick prayer-cum-oath to catch this man as a way of making amends to his departed wife and daughter.

A tannoy announcement told Marsh that his train was arriving in Birmingham New Street, his penultimate destination. He looked at his timetable and saw that he had two hours before his train to Moleshill arrived: time to briefly reacquaint himself with the city. The train drew to a halt and the scramble began as books were put away, laptops switched off and coats donned. A light screen of drizzle and low cloud had accompanied the train all the way from London. Abandoned sandwich cartons and empty paper coffee cups were strewn across the train carriage tables – no attempt being made to throw them way. Marsh wrinkled his nose at the bad manners and grabbed his briefcase. A luggage transfer service was moving his cases to the hotel where he was staying.

Marsh emerged from the subterranean train station and took in the vista of the city. He was fairly impressed with the new cityscape that greeted him. He saw the sixties behemoth that was the Rotunda still blotted the landscape.

"Nothing a few sticks of dynamite wouldn't solve, eh?" a council worker quipped cheekily as he pushed his dustcart by.

"My thoughts exactly," replied Marsh with a smile.

He ambled on into the Bull Ring and stopped for a coffee at one of the multifarious chains of coffee bars that dotted the plaza, dominated by the church of St Martin's on one side and the new Selfridges; Christianity and capitalism seemingly co-existing side-by-side.

A waitress brought Marsh his Americano; he thanked her and took out his cigar case. He nipped the end off a cigar, and lit it with his battered Ronson lighter, rolling the cigar in his hand to get an even light with the flame. He took a deep drag and exhaled a plume of blue smoke.

For a brief moment the sun came out, the wind had blown the clouds away and the plaza was lit in bright sunlight. Young families passed him by. Suddenly Marsh realised it wasn't just the architecture that had changed. When Marsh had left England in the late sixties, Birmingham had been a divided city. Signs were displayed in windows of hotels, "No Blacks or Irish". National Front graffiti was scrawled in areas where immigrants lived. Looking around at families of all colours, races and religions happily passing by made Marsh give a sigh of contentment.

He took a sip of his coffee and fished a set of folders from his case. He began reading some background notes that had arrived on his vintage fax machine a few weeks previously. Notes from a darker episode in the past, which might have a searingly present pertinence now.

# Police Headquarters, Melbourne.

James was ushered into the Commissioner's office still clutching the now three-quarters empty bottle of water that Bain had given him. He supposed that it was technically a piece of evidence.

"Take a pew," said the Commissioner, looking at James as if he were Lazarus emerging from the tomb. "Well you're a lucky bugger – not many guys come back in one piece from a drive with Cyrus Bain. When the shout went out over the comms net I thought we'd be seeing you on a slab next."

"Tell me about it," said James, sinking into a leather chair.

"Suppose one good thing has come out of this," said the Commissioner.

"What's that?"

"We know that Bain doesn't want you dead." he said with apparent concern.

James' puzzlement for this display of apparent emotion suddenly cleared when he realised his boss's relief came from his ability to stand-down James' costly round-the-clock protection.

"So things can get back to normal," said the Commissioner.

"Normal! That's a word that's been in short supply lately," retorted James.

"Sure is," said the Commissioner. "These are for you," he said, placing some items on his desk.

James stood up to look at them. One was a brand new warrant card to replace his old one, which had been singed in the plane crash, and a folder containing an open-ended return flight ticket from Melbourne to Darwin.

"You fly out at 6am tomorrow, make sure you don't come back till you've caught the bastard," said the Commissioner, giving James a firm bloke handshake. "It cost me a lot of dosh to save your English arse. Now get out there and make sure my money was well spent," he said with a fatherly overtone.

James couldn't follow that so he merely picked up the warrant card and tickets off the desk and left the office. Although he considered Melbourne as his home, a creeping admiration for the tough cops of the NT had grown on him and he couldn't help feeling like he was going back home. And he had a job to do there. His abduction and survival had filled him with renewed zeal to capture the killer… and Bain. But Bain could wait.

"Now our business is north," said James to himself.

# Crompton Airfield, Nr Chandler, Northern Territory.

Constable Dan Collins of the Northern Territory Police played steering wheel bongos to AC/DC's "All Night Long", as he sat in the cab of his pickup truck at an isolated airstrip. He tracked back over the events of the past few weeks since he'd first met Lawrence James in The Rice Bowl and how the night had ended in a blurry mess of shooters. If they could just nail this bastard it would all be alright. He'd have some good tales to tell and the scars to prove it.

What kind of mongrel would prey on defenceless women? The bars and truck stops of the territory were alive with rumours of who it might be and women rarely travelled alone after dark. If they did, they were usually armed with some weapon or other. Strangers were eyed with suspicion and the usual open welcome for tourists and outsiders had changed to a wary suspicion.

Inevitably, the matter of race had reared its ugly head and some were quick to blame the killings on an Aborigine preying on pretty white girls. Collins had been called to more than one incident where an overzealous rancher had brandished a loaded weapon at Aborigines doing nothing more suspicious than walking to town.

This had stuck in Collin's craw and he had had no qualms in confiscating the weapons from the individuals concerned. For sure, the sooner the killer was caught, the better.

He was suddenly snapped awake by a movement to the rear of his car. Instinctively, his hand reached for his Glock 17, which he was wearing in a shoulder holster. As his vision cleared, he heard the passenger door open, and he raised the gun.

"Some bloody welcome that is," said Lawrence James with a reassuring smile as he leant into the truck. "By the way, if you're planning to shoot me you'd better take the safety off first."

Both men shared a laugh. James stowed his rucksack in the back of the truck and soon the pair were tearing up the blacktop to Chandler.

"I hope you've got a black tie: you've got a funeral to go to tomorrow," said Collins. "A former copper called Sutton. Well, he kicked the bucket last weekend and they're putting him six feet under tomorrow. Caulfield wants you to tag along and see if you can get any inside track on these Brotherhood types – y'know, the Wombat Mafia or whatever they are. Don't worry, I'll lend you a tie but I'm not sure the trousers will fit you, you fat bastard – too much bloody room service and sitting on your arse in court. You better get back to work on the bags, we've got a killer to catch," he said in deadly earnest.

"Amen to that," said James, working his neck muscles whilst twisting his head in a circular motion in an effort to loosen up. The truck rumbled up the blacktop and Collins turned up the stereo.

# Old Swan Hotel, Moleshill.

Adrian Marsh mopped up the last of the tomato juice with what might have been his fifth or sixth round of toast as he sat amidst the debris of a full English breakfast. He was the sole diner in the oak-beamed room resplendent with horse brasses and all the ubiquitous ephemera of an English coaching inn. A waitress walked over and filled his coffee cup. Marsh mumbled his thanks through a mouthful of toast. Outside the window the business of the day was beginning – an electric milk float made its stately progress up the main street accompanied by a small and overgrowing number of irate commuters itching to get past in their cars.

As he folded the tomato bespattered copy of *The Times*, Marsh thought about the days ahead and of the disturbing reports he had read the night before. He had originally positioned himself in a corner of the hotel's public bar with a rather good pint of Hook Norton ale, but the noise of a football game blaring from a preposterously huge television had sent him to seek solace in his room.

Time had changed the country Marsh had known. People were better off materially, but had lost something in the process, delicacy, politeness. Equipped with a large glass of the Talisker he'd bought in the tax free shop at the airport he had stayed up till nearly two making himself familiar with the happenings of the St James' Home for Boys, a draughty and austere Victorian building which Marsh had passed during his taxi ride from the train station to the hotel. Even in the fading dusk of a summer evening the house had looked ominous and brooding, set back from the road behind high walls and wrought iron gates, large trees forming a less than welcoming backdrop. Recounting what he had read from the photocopied pages that he had been sent by

Patricia Moore, a local journalist who had spent the last few years tracing the whereabouts of the former residents.

The home had operated from the late 1950s to the early 1980s. Originally run by the council, new legislation and a lack of funds had seen the home taken over by the Catholic Church who assumed responsibility for the original inhabitants as well as furnished the home with a cadre of orphans and unwanted children from across the country.

From the outset, rumours of widespread cruelty had abounded from inside its walls. These rumours were eventually substantiated by local women who worked there as cooks and cleaners. They quickly paid the price for their loose tongues and were dismissed, their roles taken over by Carmelite nuns who were rarely seen.

Preliminary investigations into the rumours by the local council were soon scuppered as it was quickly pointed out that the council had no remit over a home run by the Catholic Archdiocese of Birmingham. A subsequent investigation carried out by this authority cleared the staff of any wrongdoing and suggested that the regime was "appropriate" to an institution dealing with "difficult children".

Nearly two decades elapsed and the home eventually closed in 1987, the remaining residents being scattered across local council children's homes and foster parents.

However, in 1995, reporter Patricia Moore began investigating the happenings at the home after covering a murder trial at Birmingham Crown Court. The defendant, Michael Pearson, who was subsequently found guilty and sentenced to life imprisonment for the abduction, rape and murder of a 10-year-old girl, claimed he had committed the act after years of mental illness compounded by years of brutal treatment and sexual abuse at the home. Using this background, Patricia Moore, against the wishes of her editor, began a one-woman campaign to find the inhabitants of the home and gather their stories. It was this woman who Marsh was due to meet at 8.30 that morning.

\*\*\*

Travel broadens the mind, they say, and you needed to broaden her mind.

She was sharp, given, but street smart, not culture smart. She could scratch your eyes out and knee you in the balls, but she didn't know how to order at a restaurant. More than a decade living in provincial Britain can do that to you.

Suicide, the coroner ruled at Martin's inquest. You'd been in the public gallery when the white-haired coroner had returned the verdict. You'd taken her with you to London. Her adopted mum bailed out one night. The police made a cursory look for her, but the consensus was that Martin had murdered her and seeing as he was dead, all things being equal, she'd never be found.

It was easy enough to take her out on a passport that cost you £500 in a Soho pub. Fortune had smiled on you that year – you'd got her back – the university had offered you redundancy and your ancient Auntie Alice who you'd faithfully written to for years had finally pegged out, leaving you a cool fifty grand.

Weighed down with cash, you and your new daughter had spent a year travelling the well-trodden tourist routes from Paris through Europe, into Asia through Turkey and onto the Far East. Making up for lost time, sharing new places and spending time together. Sharing new experiences, but maybe not all of them. She hadn't been keen to "do that" again.

But you had the need, the fixation and being a tourist in anonymous cities gave you the chance to hunt and disappear without trace. It wasn't like the old days – you wanted to be in the limelight – getting your column inches, taunting the cops. If they caught you, what could they do, keep you in prison for the rest of your life? You'd still get three meals a day, books and visits.

Not that it mattered, really, you'd died a long time ago, amidst the smell of incense and candles as the crucified Christ looked down impotently from the cross.

But now a long running bird had come home to roost, giving you the opportunity to ensure a little earthly justice caught up with your tormentor, in case there was no hereafter.

# Palmer's Cross, Northern Territory.

The cops are a large family and like most families only come together in large numbers in times of trial or celebration. And, like families, the members sometimes need to do things out of duty and familial obligation, rather than desire.

It was the latter that brought most police officers attending the funeral of Murray Sutton, as they sweated in the dress uniforms in the pews of the Sacred Heart Catholic Church.

There were only half a dozen, most of them silver-haired members of the old guard – pot-bellied Constables or Sergeants who, content with their lot, had meandered through their careers and were just waiting for retirement.

James scratched at his neck as the tie he had borrowed from Johnson threatened to cut off his breathing and the cheap polyester shirt he'd bought from a supermarket itched his skin, clinging to his back as he sweated in the mid-morning heat.

The elderly priest launched into a eulogy, making the most out of the material he had to work with, a mediocre cop who married his childhood sweetheart and they had a couple of kids. Even Sutton's duty as a cop had been tainted, a career of looking the other way and brown envelopes stuffed with dirty money. Thankfully, the service was relatively short and after the eulogy and a couple of hymns the priest gave Sutton his final send-off. The congregation began filtering out from the dark interior of the church into the scorching heat and intense light of a Northern Territory day.

Throughout the service James had felt someone's eyes boring into the back of his head. Maybe he was being paranoid, but he couldn't help a surreptitious glance over his shoulder. Out of the corner of his eye, he saw a man wearing a worn blazer and tie looking right in his direction, not with malice, but definite interest. James made a mental note to check the guy out after the service.

A gathering was being held in a nearby pub. James sauntered over there and grabbed a beer and a curling ham sandwich. He wolfed it down and followed it with a glug of beer. His appetite sated, he ripped the top of a packet of Lucky Strikes and made for the front door. Making small talk about what a nice guy Sutton had been wasn't on his agenda. James walked out of the pub and sat down on a low wall bordering the large rectangle of tarmac that served as the pub's car park.

Call it cop instinct, a keen sense of self-preservation or what you like, but without looking around James knew the guy was there. Then he realised what had happened. It was the smell of Old Spice carried on the breeze that had caused him to turn. A childhood smell. His old man usually had a couple of bottles of it on the go. To James, Old Spice meant staying at Grandma's overnight while his parent went to a party or some work event. His old man, unusually wearing a suit, would always splash a dash on himself before leaving. He'd had it good, he supposed. Better memories of his old man than Bain had. Still, plenty of people had it rough, doesn't mean that you had to go nuts and become a criminal. His train of thought was broken by a low voice.

"Can't say I cared much for that bastard, but a free feed, a free feed eh, and there'll be grog involved. You're onto a winner."

James turned his cigarette, quickly transferred it to his mouth, his hands at his sides, leaning on the balls of his feet, loose and ready for action.

"Steady on fella – I only wanted to shoot the breeze and cadge a smoke. I suppose you're a cop – but you don't have cop written all over you. Yet," said the man in the blazer.

James recognised the man from the church, probably in his mid to late fifties. He had a good head of hair and hadn't got fat like many of his peers, but he had a drinker's nose, blistered and red. The smell of Old Spice was stronger now but it didn't mask the smell of beer on his breath and the slight glazed look in the guy's eye, which James had learned to read when he was a beat cop in England. It meant you had a slight physical and mental advantage over the other guy, whose judgements and reactions were dinted by booze.

"Mr Baz Twomlow, if I'm not mistaken," said James, proffering a hand.

"Got me in one, copper," the man said, squeezing James' hand in a friendly shake.

James recognised Twomlow from a framed picture in Marsh's house, taken in the seventies at a newspaper office. Five or six young guys in shirts, sleeves rolled up, kipper ties askew, looking earnestly up from their desks in a newsroom – their electronic typewriters in front of them, full ashtrays to the sides of them.

"You were Adrian Marsh's boss at the *Telegraph*, is that right?"

"It is indeed, Officer, you got me, it's a fair cop," said Twomlow.

"Lawrence James, Victoria Police," James said.

"What you doing in this neck of the woods and what you doing trailing behind that old hack Marsh for?" asked Twomlow.

"Well, it's confidential, but you can probably piece the jigsaw together yourself," said James.

"The bloody Dingo, I should have known," exclaimed Twomlow. "Say, I might be able to put a few things straight with you on that score. I got a tab running at the Waldorf down the street there. We could uncork a good Beaujolais and toast that piece of shit Sutton," he said, the prospect of having an excuse to not drink alone lighting up his eyes.

Marsh and Twomlow had once been good friends, but like most chronic alcoholics Twomlow had burned much of the goodwill Marsh had felt for him over the years and the two men had drifted apart.

"Sounds like a plan," said James, calculating the odds cynically. Twomlow would probably end up getting blotto with or without James, but he might also really have something to tell. James decided to play the long game.

The Waldorf's real name was the Como Inn – a three-star affair that sat on the main street and played host to businessmen on the way to Darwin and coming back from Alice Springs. It had a reasonable menu and a well-stocked cocktail bar. It was named the Waldorf after Kyle Dorfe, an American who had stopped in the town in 1980 and had never left after buying the hotel, which had been boarded up for five years. In a couple of years he'd got it back up and running and it had become a stop-off point for tourists, but also a watering hole for locals like Twomlow.

The two men made their way into the bar and seated themselves in a booth with vinyl seats. A young waitress brought them a wine list and placed it in front of Twomlow.

"I'll take a bottle of Château Petanque '85 please, love – and two glasses," he said, without looking at the menu.

A few minutes later she brought the bottle and two glasses out to them. Twomlow poured a small glass, sniffed it and swirled it around and then took a small sip. He washed it around in his mouth for a while and then swallowed.

"That'll do nicely," he said, pouring a glass each for them. "So, you want to know a little bit about why Adie was called off the drink-driving story, eh? Well you've picked the right time. I've got a granddaughter in Perth who needs a grandpa and not one who's soused all the while. I'm getting out of town next week, and I'm going to Perth and checking into a drying out clinic. So, I might as well burn my bridges for sure, eh, Lawrence, whaddya say?" he said with a wink, draining his glass and looking James square in the face.

"I'm all ears," said James.

He felt his scalp itch and a tingle of suspense run down his spine. It was the same feeling he'd has as a child when Mrs Bailey began reading the class a new story or when a new tale began on television's *Jackanory*. James knew he'd backed the right pony. He took a big drink of wine and began to listen.

# Chandler, Northern Territory.

Jenny Somerville and Edgar Wallace were the only two tourists in the bar. But they wouldn't have called themselves tourists: they were travellers with the battered rucksacks and Facebook albums loaded with pictures to prove it. Vietnam, Laos, Thailand, Burma – or Myanmar, as the gangster generals who ran the place like their personal fiefdom would have it called.

Either way, the pair had been there, done that and got the proverbial t-shirt. Not that the pair would be as crass as to buy t-shirts: that was definitely for tourists. One of the things that had drawn them together was their loathing of tourists whom they saw as the antithesis of their philosophy of travelling. That is to tread lightly and not leave footprints. They travelled on public transport, ate local and stayed in accommodation that avoided the cardboard cut-out hotels. This is how they had come to find The Fat Wombat.

Not that money was a problem for either of them. Edgar Wallace, just into his thirties, had sold his computer games company for a small fortune. The business, which he had spent seven years building up, began from a side project he had started during his second year of a university degree in French and Literature. Edgar had been one of a few entrepreneurs that had turned the Midlands town of Leamington Spa into a mini Silicon Valley. On the day he left, the town boasted no less than twenty games developers.

Wallace had been on his way to a conference in London when he'd spotted the brunette bob of hair that belonged to Jenny Somerville, an eighteen-year-old Oxford girl who had been to an open day at Warwick University. Far from being the archetypal socially inept computer boffin, Edgar brimming with confidence, had approached her and struck up a conversation. Before they arrived in Oxford he had her phone number.

The rest, they say, is history and now they sat in the midst of a table strewn with the debris of breakfast. Edgar had gone for breakfast "with the lot". The more calorie-conscious Jenny had opted for a bowl of porridge and chopped fruit. Edgar was buried in his MacBook, quietly bemoaning the woeful lack of speed from the wireless broadband.

Seeing that Edgar was going nowhere fast, Jenny felt cantankerous and tapped Edgar playfully on the head, stood up and said, "I'm off to get some fags. I'll be back in five minutes."

He heard the slip-slap of her flip-flops and the chime of the door as she left.

She wasn't five minutes or fifty for that matter. He'd gotten buried in a swathe of emails. Edgar had mistakenly believed that selling the business would have given him freedom. He'd thought that the freedom from the fifty- to sixty-hour weeks and not holding a formal position would mean freedom. It had not. Now he had divested himself of the company everyone wanted a piece of him. Much like the advertising and software sectors, the games development industry was all about people. There were partnerships, families and feuds that would make the antipathy between the Montagues and the Capulets look like a dispute over a shared drive. Edgar had received a bunch of offers for roles at top companies.

His Blackberry buzzed, the red light flickering like a warning beacon on top of a tall building. Red light means danger. He looked at the dial of his Brietling. She'd been gone for over an hour. A sort of sixth sense kicked in. Suddenly, he thought of Jenny in danger. He dropped forty dollars onto the table, folded the screen of his MacBook and pocketed his Blackberry. Clutching the computer under his arm he ran into the street and looked both ways. Something told him *left*.

The street was quiet, traffic was steady and pedestrians thinly spread along the streets. He jogged slowly to a junction and saw in a car park a VW Combivan, Jenny loved them and they had been talking about buying one. That's where she was. He saw her brunette hair poking out from under her bandanna that she always wore to stop the sun bleaching it. She was talking to someone inside the van and had one foot on the sill where the side door opened. A man stood nearby, but out of her peripheral vision. A truck carrying pallets of timber lumbered past, throwing up a swirl of red dust causing him to raise his hands in front of his face as the dust choked him and made him cough. The truck rolled up the street and his vision came back. He looked at the scene and his brain made the link before his vision could confirm what he already knew.

Jenny's bandanna lay on the dusty pavement. The van's door was sliding shut and someone was behind the wheel, the engine revving. He broke into a run and soon cleared the gap quickly. He heard a muffled squeal from inside; he wrenched the side door open and tried to get a foot on the sill. The van screeched to a halt. He was pulling himself up into the van when a searing pain, shot through his chest. He fell to the ground and the van roared off. The noise had by this time attracted several people, including a waiter from The Fat Wombat who'd been looking for Edgar who'd left his expensive leather holdall behind. The waiter bent down towards the prostrate young man and leant down to him. Edgar rolled over and raised his arms. A puddle of bright crimson stayed on the pavement, his linen shirt soaked from the blood pumping from the single stab wound through his aorta.

"Fuck me, he's been stabbed!" shouted the man to the five or six bystanders. The crowd jostled around.

"Call an ambulance, someone for God's sake," a woman screeched. A fat, sweating businessman punched some numbers into his mobile phone.

"Call the cops, too, I think they stole his computer," said another person.

An ambulance arrived and the paramedics strapped Edgar to a stretcher, onto a gurney and into the ambulance. They'd known he was past help, but hadn't wanted to alarm the crowd. Taking a final reading of his vitals, they phoned in and declared him dead just after 11.17am. There was a buzzing sound from the recently deceased young man's pocket. "One unread message". The red light on the Blackberry flashed red, but the lights on the heart and breathing monitor showed flat lines.

Back at The Fat Wombat, the shocked bystanders were being treated to complimentary pastries and coffee. For those most affected, generous measures of brandy had been discreetly added. Two uniform cops were taking statements. The consensus had been that Edgar had been the victim of a mugging gone wrong or a fight over drugs maybe.

It was only several hours after the incident had occurred that they got to talk to Jason Douglas, the owner of The Fat Wombat. The by now jaded cops were taking his statement when his eyes glanced down on a small backpack which seemed to have no owner.

"Bloody hell, he was here with a girl, a pretty young brunette," one man said. The tension built.

"Shit, they were taking the girl… he was trying to stop them," another person added.

A murmur of excitement ran through the café to be replaced all too soon by an ominous silence.

# Moleshill, United Kingdom.

The less than conversational taxi driver dropped Marsh off at the semi-detached house on the cul-de-sac at the edge of the town. Marsh paid off the cabbie, not wanting his surly company on the return journey. He had memorised the route from the hotel and realised he could walk.

The curtains were drawn upstairs, as were the blinds downstairs, casting a drab appearance. The lawn was shabby and unkempt. He opened the wonky wooden gate and jumped back as a shaggy ginger cat squeezed through the gap and ran across the road. The door opened a crack and a figure peered out.

"Adrian Marsh?" said a woman's voice.

"The very same," said Marsh, cracking a smile. He detected a relaxation in her mood.

"Excuse me a minute," she said. The door closed, there was a rattle, the chain was removed and the door opened. A woman in her late forties opened the door. She wore jeans and a baggy jumper, but despite this Marsh saw a svelte female figure and felt a murmur of carnal stirrings he'd not felt for a long time.

Marsh realised he'd been caught out, took a step back and pushed out a hand. "Glad to meet you," he said.
"Patricia Moore, former news editor of the *Birmingham Post* and known locally as the 'crazy cat woman'," she said with a weary frown, absent-mindedly plucking a cat hair from her jumper and flicking it out into the garden. "Well, come in and I'll sort you a coffee."

"That'd be great thanks, although the stuff at the hotel was good," said Marsh.

"A coffee connoisseur?" she raised an eyebrow. "I thought you Aussies just swilled beer all day?"

"Well, as I'm originally from Surrey, I guess that explains it," laughed Marsh.

"Get away – you're so Australian all you'd need is a koala round your neck and a hat with corks." Her face lit up a little. "Come through to the kitchen and we can talk there."

She moved through the hall which was stacked with shoe-boxes and box files, loose leaves of papers sticking from underneath the lids. Moore caught his glance.

"My Black Archive – I'll explain later."

She spooned coffee into the percolator, and leant over the sink to fill the jug with water. Marsh averted his eyes and tried to strike up a conversation.

"So you got into all this because of Michael Pearson?" Marsh asked.

"That happened to be the thin end of the wedge, but it's as good a place to start as any."

Marsh heard the coffee gurgling into the jug and in a sort of Pavlovian reaction he began to get the urge for a cigar and patted his pocket.

"I was thinking that, too," said Moore, waving a packet of Marlboro Red cigarettes. Marsh took out his cigar case and battered Ronson. "We can take our coffee in the garden; it's not raining for the moment," she said.

She pulled out a large bunch of keys and undid three locks on an internal security shutter.

"Like Alcatraz, eh?" she quipped, slotting another key into the French doors. "Another thing I'll need to explain, I suppose."

She wrenched the French doors open and a gush of fresh air shifted the stale air, which smelt of dust and cat hair.

"Go and take a seat. I'll bring the coffee out," she said, pointing to the garden.

Marsh went past her; she made a small effort to get out of his way. As he brushed past her, he caught a smell of shampooed hair, a delicate feminine smell he hadn't smelt for a long time.

"Well trained, aren't you?" she quipped. They exchanged smiles.

Marsh crossed a well-manicured lawn and walked onto a gravelled pathway. The back garden was much neater and well protected, he noted – an eight-foot wooden fence with razor wire discreetly running across the top. He took himself up onto a raised piece of garden and sat in a small wooden pagoda walled in on three sides and roofed in from the elements. He sat down and assembled his smoking paraphernalia on the wooden table. He heard clattering from the kitchen and suddenly felt a tremendous surge of well-being. Marsh had cut and lit his cigar and was sending a plume of blue smoke skywards, when Moore clattered out with a tray of coffee.

"Brought the jug, we'll probably need it. I've got a lot to share with you," she said.

"Well, I've got nowhere to go and this is a big cigar," he said with a flourish. She smiled back and folded her arms.

"You know, I used to think people who smoked those were wankers, you know, with size issues, like some sort of phallic compensation. But maybe they were just wankers. So far you're changing my mind," she said.

"It's early days yet, so wait and see," replied Marsh. "I'll pour; you talk," he said, picking up the jug.

"It was 1995; I had been promoted to news editor on the *Post*, not exactly breaking the glass ceiling, but good enough. Anyway, my mum was still alive at the time and a full-blown Catholic.

"So, one week, after the Sunday service I always attended with her, there's a coffee, tea and biscuits affair in the parish hall where my mum used to go for a chin-wag. I used to take my coffee and smoke a cigarette outside.

"One day I was doing this and a guy was standing across the road from the church. He came over and asked me for a cigarette. He was casually dressed and didn't smell or anything, but he had an odd air about him, something restless. He told me he used to be a Catholic but he thought it was all shit now. I told him something similar just to break the silence. He told me he was a carpenter. I told him he I was a journalist on the *Post.*"

She paused, lit a cigarette and a far-off look came into her eyes. "Which you could say was one of the smartest or stupidest things I could have done," she said.

"I think you did the right thing," said Marsh with a reassuring smile.

Patricia Moore stirred her coffee absent-mindedly. "So, we were standing outside the church, he's not half way down his fag, when these two big guys came up. They're parishioners; they were builders or something. 'Is this man bothering you, Miss Moore?' they asked me. 'Nah, he's fine,' I said, feeling a bit stupid for sticking up for a guy I didn't know.

"'Father Donnelly told you there's nothing here for you, so take off, if you know what's good for you,' said one of the blokes.

"The man flicked his fag into the weeds by the wall, said 'Ta for the smoke,' and took off.

"One of the parishioners said, 'That toerag's been hanging round the vestry up to no good. Father Donnelly's been finding him in the church at all odd hours, so we thought we'd have a word.'

"'Fair enough,' I said. And I thought nothing more of it. Until a few weeks later I was at work and the concierge rang me telling me there was a guy in reception who wanted to talk to me. He said he knew me from church. The concierge was used to dealing with weirdoes who dropped in with tall tales and asked me if I wanted him to get rid of the guy. I'd just put the first edition to bed and was looking to stretch my legs, grab a coffee and a fag, so I thought, *What the hell.*

"I grabbed my coat and pad and went downstairs to meet him. He was sitting in the foyer and looked a mess. He looked like he'd been sleeping rough, and had a black eye and nasty looking split lip. 'Your friends from the church. So much for fucking hospitality,' he said. The concierge was hovering and I felt like this was the wrong place and the wrong time, so I took him to a café. I bought him a fry-up and he told me his life story.

"By the time he'd finished, I'd filled my pad and my coffee had gone cold. It wasn't a happy beginning and it didn't seem he was going to have a happy ending. He told me he'd been brought up in a home and the priests and others had 'done things' to him. He'd left the home but couldn't get a decent job because he lacked qualifications. He'd gone to London and ended up on the streets sniffing glue to take away the memories. He'd done a couple of short stretches in prison for burglary and shoplifting. He told me what the priests had done to him, had messed him up sexually and he couldn't form relationships with women or even male friends for that matter. Then he'd have these strange urges for younger girls, voices telling him to hurt them, stuff like that. He'd been to his GP and gotten referred to mental health services – after an eighteen-month wait. He got some counselling sessions and a prescription for some anti-psychotics, but chuff all else.

"I gave him £20, gave him my work telephone number and told him I'd look into it. To be honest I put him down as another Hard Luck Harry – believe me I'd seen my share of them. I did a spot of digging in the clippings library. But there was nothing in print, just unsubstantiated rumours that had done the rounds for years. That was all."

She poured some more coffee into her cup and stubbed her cigarette out into the ashtray.

"So you had a great lead but no tangible evidence," said Marsh, exhaling smoke from a corner of his mouth.

"Well, for a short while, but I soon got much more than I bargained for," said Moore, shifting in her seat. "I was on the night shift, back in the day when there were still decent staffing levels and circulation to go with it. Usually it meant dialling all three emergency services every few hours and seeing who'd been maimed, murdered, mugged or shot."

"Been there myself too many times. Bet you never had any fatalities due to kangaroos, though?" said Marsh. They shared a much needed laugh.

"I was there half asleep when my phone rings, it's him. By now I've got his name from the cops, Michael Pearson.

"The back-door channels had told us he was a 'weirdo' and possibly a paedo – he'd been picked up getting a little too close to a middle school apparently. 'I need your help,' he tells me – 'I'm gonna do something stupid if you don't help, you've gotta get me locked up. Tonight!' I wrote down the address of the phone box that he'd called from and made my way there. He was in an agitated state. I drove him to a police station and we spoke to the duty sergeant. He told me there was nothing he could do. It was a Saturday night, the cells were full of drunks, the psychiatrists would be back in on Monday and he hadn't actually done anything, so what could he do. Then things turned ugly. 'What about this, cunt!' he shouted and threw a small bag of cocaine at the cop behind the window. The cop got angry; two others came from behind him and threw him out into the street. I just stood there. The duty sergeant made me a cup of tea and we talked things over. The cop's hands were tied. He hadn't done anything wrong and they weren't social services, and that was that."

The tears welled up in Moore's eyes and she began to cry, bucket loads of tears. Her hand shook. Marsh grabbed it and held it. Her jaw quivered as she spoke.

"The next Tuesday he was found walking along the canal carrying a bloody knife and some items of a girl's school uniform. Julie Golding. You know the rest."

"Unfortunately, I do," said Marsh. His hand stayed where it was.

"So after the trial, I backed his appeal, not that he was not guilty, but that he wasn't fit to stand trial. But these nuances are beyond the British public and it made me as popular as a leper. I went to see him in prison and recorded a lot of tapes of what happened to him – you can borrow some copies I've made. It soon became clear it hadn't just been him and that it went higher than a renegade priest. The abuse was systematic and the operation to cover up what happened had gone high up in the archdiocese.

It turned out our Father Donnelly had been one of the good guys – he'd not touched any of the kids. And he'd also got Pearson some money in a tacit form of compensation," she said, swirling the remains of her cold coffee.

"So you didn't get any help from your editor?" asked Marsh. "Nope, not a thing. But things soon built to a head anyway. I really didn't have time to be fighting office politics with a misogynist dinosaur like him. Plus, he was halfway up the arse of the Archbishop of Birmingham, anyway – the West Midlands version of *Opus Dei*."

"So you got the push?" asked Marsh.

"Voluntary redundancy, they called it. Pretty generous too, I think they hoped I'd bugger off to the sun and give up the trail. I'd heard of other people being bought off. So I paid off some of the mortgage and put up a fence it was less easy to throw dog shit over and got an un-kickable front door."

"The Alcatraz doors?" asked Marsh.

"They came later, thanks to my new friend who I'm getting to, if you give me a chance," she said.

"Sorry I'm chock full of caffeine and nicotine and can't sit still," said Marsh.

"Well, it was late autumn 1995 and things weren't going well. That's bit of a porky really, as the investigation was going well. I had been burgled for the third time and was cleaning the human excrement off the walls where it had been smeared. In retrospect, I see the burglaries as a positive. Someone wanted me to stop and they were prepared to do quite a bit to stop me. Anyway, I digress. I was wiping the shit off the wall when the phone rang. It shocked me, as I was ex-directory after having a torrent of abusive calls calling me a paedo lover. I'd put together a PO Box and a freephone number, which went to an answering service when it rang through. Only about six people had my number then. I wiped my hands as best as I could.

"'Patricia Moore?' a voice asked. 'Depends who's asking,' I did in my best tough gal voice. 'My name is Jonathan Swift, a partner at Widdecombe & Croft, in Birmingham – I was given this number by a Mr M Pearson, who said you would be happy to speak to me about a client who has approached me on a very sensitive issue. In a nutshell, he's willing to help your case on the grounds that you use me as an intermediary and his details are not made public. Would you be able to meet me at our offices in Newhall Street tomorrow afternoon?' So, I was intrigued – I agreed and along I went."

Moore shifted in her seat. "I've gotta go for a wee. We've been here a fair while and there's still much more to tell," she said standing up. "How about an early lunch and maybe a cocktail?"

"Suits me," said Marsh, watching as she disappeared through the doors.

He took a long pull on his cigar and blew a plume of smoke skywards. Of all the places he'd thought getting involved with James would bring him, here was not one of them. They were on the trail of a cold-blooded killer, he knew. But he couldn't pretend he wasn't enjoying it and maybe Moore had something to do with that.

# Unknown location, Northern Territory.

Jenny Somerville was sick as a pike and felt like a pig had shat in her head. She had a desperate thirst and needed the toilet urgently. The two lines from the film *Withnail and I* about the pig and the pike, caused her to laugh to herself. The small laugh echoed around the chamber she found herself in. The laugh also heartened her and the despair she had initially felt melted away.

She had never been religious, but she believed in a higher power, even if it was only an extension of one's own consciousness that allowed you to remove yourself from your own immediate thoughts and transcend to a higher plane. She had first become aware of this feeling during the entrance exams for Queen Anne's Girls' School, when she was eight.

It had remained dormant until a particularly difficult English Literature exam, not that the exam was hard for Jenny: just that she could not decide between questions three or five. The voice had told her five and she had passed with an A*.

This same feeling of zen-like calm took over now. She wondered how many times she and Edgar had watched *Withnail and I*. Even on their trip they had watched it several times, on tropical beaches, beside camp fires. *I want to watch it, and I will do so again,* she told herself. But first, to escape. She took in her surroundings.

She was sitting upright on a thin camping mattress. Her hands were cuffed, but there was a chain between the bracelets about 30cm long which gave her some freedom of movement. Her legs were manacled, too. Both sets of cuffs ran to a chain around her waist which was in turn padlocked to a ring fastened into the wall. She got up and did some stretches, thinking that the more she sat and pondered the quicker her mind and body would atrophy to the submissiveness of a captive.

She walked to the end of the semi-dark chamber; some natural light was stealing in through a grate high in the ceiling. She shuffled across the concrete floor to the door. It was steel, looked around two to three inches thick and had no handle on the inside. It reminded Jenny of doors she had seen on films on submarines and in bunkers. *That is where I am,* she realised. *I'm in a bunker.*

Edgar had gone on at great length about the fact that loads of US soldiers were stationed in the area during World War Two. Nobody would find her here unless she got out herself. She walked back to the thin mattress and sat down. Next to the mattress were two buckets with lids. "Pee and poo, I suppose?" she said to herself. She moved the buckets to the other end of the room and then made use of the facilities.

She went back to the mattress and sat down. There was a cardboard box by the wall. The first item she drew out was a packet of antiseptic hand wipes. *A feminine touch?* thought Jenny. She wiped her hands and looked again inside the cardboard box. She took out three one-litre bottles of still water and a box which seemed to contain food.

She pulled the cap off one of the waters and glugged down half a bottle of water. The bottles were branded but had no seals which was strange, she thought.

She realised she'd probably been drugged as she had no recall of how she got here. Her last cogent memory had been sitting with a huge mug of coffee. The memory brought her back to her immediate hunger, now she had slaked her thirst. She tore open the box. It contained a pizza, veggie by the look of it. There was also a box of chicken pieces and several lidded containers. She pulled a slice of pizza off and began eating it. With her free hand she pulled the lid off the pots. Potato salad and coleslaw. She paused for a second in mid-chew. Perhaps the food was drugged?

Perhaps it was, but then why bother drugging her again now she was safely in the dungeon?

Plus if she didn't eat, she would soon grow weak and lethargic, becoming a more pliable prisoner. She realised that this was something she could not afford. First she would eat and then she would think about how to escape.

She was not done for yet.

# Chandler Police Station, Northern Territory.

The Incident Room was full to the brim with detectives wearing a variety of civilian clothes. Some of them just looked like they had stepped out of a GAP advert. Others wore baggy shorts and vests. A variety of tattoos were on display, from straightforward names and Celtic crosses to more elaborate snakes and elfish women adorning a whole arm. Others bore military symbols reminiscent of recent time spent in Afghanistan and the Australian army.

The Northern Territory Police provided a safe harbour for capable men looking to continue the comradeship they had left behind. Better than a desk job in civvy street, descent into the bottom of a bottle or escape via a syringe.

Uniformed cops, dusty and sweat-stained, traipsed in like a parade of wraiths, tired but doggedly determined to keep manning the roadblocks, combing isolated outbuildings and taking numerous statements. The catering staff had made a Herculean effort to keep the coffee and food coming through the night to keep the weary cops on their toes.

A hush fell over the room as the lights went up and James and Sandersen entered the room. James looked tanned and relaxed, dapper in a linen suit. This change had not gone unnoticed by the cops in the team. They barely recognised James as the rumpled, unshaven man who had arrived a few weeks earlier. Sandersen stood by his side wearing a two-piece business suit. James picked up a spoon and a water glass and tapped it to get the assembled throng's attention. "Okay, everyone, listen up," shouted James.

The plea seemed to fall on deaf ears. Sandersen picked up a mike and let the room have a savage squeal of feedback.

"It's time to stop fucking around. This isn't a social gathering, so shut the fuck up and listen," shouted Sandersen, in a most unladylike fashion. It had the desired effect.

"Err, thanks, Ms Sandersen," said James, looking slightly shell-shocked himself. "So, let's just update you with what's happened over the past twenty-four hours." James flicked the controller and displayed a picture of a young couple standing in front of Uluru.

"Edgar Wallace, thirty-four, was stabbed to death in Yukon Street yesterday by assailant or assailants unknown. His girlfriend, Jenny Somerville, aged 25, was abducted in Yukon Street. Witnesses saw her talking to two people in a VW Camper van.

"It seems they were in the act of abducting her when Wallace intervened and got stabbed straight in the aorta. Whoever stabbed him knew what to do with a knife. And while I know a young man has been murdered, the young woman is possibly still alive and has to remain our priority. We have some grainy footage of the abduction. It was taken by accident by a tourist who was checking their battery life and was just sweeping up and down the street.

"We can thank Officer Johnson for putting the word about to all officers to ask everyone who was giving a statement to look at their phones and digital stills and video cameras for possible clues. It's been couriered by chopper to Darwin for enhanced analysis. We can pretty much assume the killers had parked the van deliberately out of view of any camera as Yukon Street had no cameras in stores or other places. It suggests a high level of professionalism and planning," said James, pausing to take a sip of water.

Sandersen, taking advantage of James' pause and the fact that he had put down the remote, jumped in. "What it also points to is that any detail, however unimportant it may seem, could be vital. So, whatever it is, put it onto CrimIN and let it decide if it's unimportant or not. Let it play Sherlock Holmes for us." CrimIN was a state-of-the-art database which analysed raw data and provided information about the possible behaviour of an offender.

"We think we've got a window of another forty-eight hours to find our victim. Our killer has held his victims for around seventy-two hours previously. We can only hope that he retains his prior MO," said Sandersen. "So, ladies and gentlemen, hop to it and let's send this young girl back safe to her parents."

She switched off the projector screens and the group broke up.

James and Sandersen made their way back to the office which had been requisitioned for them, off the same corridor as the Commissioner's. James had returned the previous evening from Melbourne. He and Sandersen had kissed briefly and then gotten straight down to a case review in light of the new evidence after the abduction of Jenny Somerville.

Jez Walker had been released without charge, shaken but now determined to abandon his book and start a non-fiction work on the Dingo case. It had been informally agreed that if and when the case was successfully concluded, he would have first-hand access to all those involved. This had proved a great motivating factor in his willingness to drop a proposed case against the NT Police for wrongful arrest. The idea had been planted in his head by a lawyer who had approached him in the street as he left the rear of the police station. How the guy had heard about his arrest was anyone's guess.

James had acknowledged that Sandersen's theory about an accomplice had been correct all along. In hindsight much of this had been borne out by the evidence. Almost all of the victims had disappeared in mysterious circumstances from venues crowded with people. Autopsies had shown that violence had not been used to subdue them as they were abducted, although traces of Rohypnol and chloroform had been found in two of the victims' bloodstreams. While James and Sandersen agreed that The Dingo had an accomplice, the manner in which this person was involved was not clear.

"It's a woman or girl, that's for sure – it's how he gets close to the victims," Sandersen said as she spooned out beef chow mein onto a plate. The Chinese food had been brought in to avoid either of the two being spotted by the gaggle of journalists who now infested the town.

"For sure," said James, deftly slicing a spring roll. "But are we thinking she's being coerced or a willing accomplice?" he asked, spearing half of the spring roll and devouring it.

"She's a willing accomplice: think about the logistics otherwise. Even if he's got a gun, he's got to eat and sleep. If they turned on him, it's game over. And look at the depth of surveillance that's been carried out. One person loitering about in any of these towns, despite all the tourists, would stand out," said Sandersen.

"So we've got a Brady and Hindley situation, then?" James said, referring to the notorious British killers, Myra Hindley and Ian Brady, who had abducted and murdered five children in the 1960s.

The thought sent a shiver down James' spine. He'd been on some tough cases, but the Moors murders, as they came to be known, had cast a long shadow over his eighties childhood. The names of Brady and Hindley had become a byword for evil and the pair had never fully been erased from his imagination. The fact that Hindley and Brady had recorded the torture and abuse of their child victims had struck him to the marrow. Even after their imprisonment they had continued to play cat-and-mouse with the authorities over the location of the grave of one of their victims.

James updated Sandersen with all he had learned from Baz Twomlow during their epic drinking bout at the Waldorf Hotel.

He outlined how The Brotherhood had run the Northern Territory with impunity. The kingpin had been one Terry Hancock, a construction millionaire and self-styled Aussie "battler".

He had somehow married a pretty and intelligent wife called Deborah, originally from the UK. They had met in Paris while she was studying French literature at the Sorbonne. Terry was at a construction conference and she was doing some translation work for the Australian Chamber of Commerce.

They had married after a whirlwind romance and Terry had brought his dream wife back to Ptarmigan. The dream had soon turned sour. Terry had reverted to his tomcat ways, having indiscreet liaisons with women half his age. He expected Deborah to play the role of little wifie and amuse herself with the Bridge Club and the Watercolour Society.

Instead, she found solace in the arms of an unknown academic who wore a sports jacket with leather elbow patches and drove a fancy car, according to Twomlow. All he knew for sure was that the unknown man had been the one stopped at the roadblock and that Deborah Hancock had disappeared for over a year, ostensibly to begin a PhD.

The couple had never divorced but led virtually separate lives, Deborah spending much of her time working with Aboriginals via the foundation she had set up with Terry's money. She was coming back to the neo-gothic pile on the outskirts of Ptarmigan the following day and James was going to speak to her and hopefully fill in some missing gaps.

"Sounds like a plan. You off to bed?" asked Sandersen.

"Yeah, I'm bushed. I might try and wade through the press clippings first: that'll be good bedtime reading, no doubt," he said. He got up, hugged Sandersen a little harder than normal and kissed her.

"See you in four," she said, as he strolled down the corridor. They had been taking four hours off to sleep, the amount strictly necessary to keep mind and body together but not much more.

James turned the key in the lock of the office he had taken up residence in. There was nothing to discern it from a regular office save for the army camp bed and the sleeping bag rolled up on it. James hung up his jacket and took off his shoes, socks and suit trousers, hanging the trousers on a coat rack. He slumped into an office chair and uttered a deep sigh. He stretched and pushed his feet into the floor and his arms above his head in an effort to unravel the knottiness he felt.

Opening a drawer he fished out a bottle of Glenfiddich and poured himself a decent slug. He took a mouthful, swilled it around his mouth and swallowed; enjoying the complex peaty taste on his tongue and the pleasant warming sensation as the scotch wormed its way down his throat. He put the glass down and began riffling through the pile of press cuttings harvested from the Australian media and beyond. Both the Melbourne *Age* and *The Sydney Morning Herald* had despatched their heavy hitters to cover the story. The British press had also sent correspondents.

James thought it fortunate that the *News of the World* had come to a sticky end as this was just the story that they would have loved. Sensationalism sells, though, and the easily decipherable idea of vulnerable, white middle-class British girls being abducted and murdered in the heart of this savage land gave the journos a field day. Even the normally middle-of-the-road *Sunday Times* had given over four pages to the story. Aside from the interviews with those directly involved in the case, there were articles given over to UK travel agents who reported that youngsters were leaving Australia in droves, and flights to Australia were taking on *Mary Celeste*-like qualities. Under the headline "The Triangle of Terror" a lavish graphic of the three towns of Ptarmigan, Boxwood and Chandler were mapped out with the locations of the bodies highlighted.

Another column spouted "Inside the mind of The Dingo". James nearly choked on his whisky. It was a piece by Sandersen. Then, the penny dropped. It would be impossible for Australia's leading expert on serial killers to go out of circulation without arousing great suspicion. James finished his scotch, set his phone's alarm clock, stretched out on his army cot and was soon slipping into sleep. As he did, he saw an image of a man in flares, a salmon pink shirt, kipper tie and a sports jacket with leather elbow patches.

His face was concealed by an apple, just like the painting by Magritte.

\*\*\*

Leather elbow patches, the pipe – a high quality Davidoff, the very best coupled with the best blend of tobacco, Virginian and Kentucky leaf, a big cup of Colombian coffee and the first pipe bowl of the day.

"Happiness is a warm (pipe) bowl," you'd written in your diary.

Marcia had called you a pathetic loser with your "phoney phallic symbols" and your "penis extension" car. But you'd stopped listening to her bullshit long ago. Plus, you knew it worked – the girls from the uni loved the jacket, the pipe and the car... and your cock, it seemed. A quick ring from a telephone box on the edge of campus, a roar along the blacktop touching 200kph got them wet. You fucked them on the leather back seat of the Pontiac.

Animal fucking, you rarely got to get your clothes off. It wasn't just the young undergrads either; the postgrads came on to you, too. A decade of kids and Saturday night beer-infused sex, made them hungry for a bit of something more carnal. You were happy to oblige. You got home at all hours stinking of sweat and other women, covered in scratches and bite-marks. Marcia didn't seem to notice or care. Every fuck on the back seat exorcised the demons, every crashing orgasm another sliver of catharsis.

Leather... a settee in the vestry, easy to wipe down, they'd thought of everything, and also no reason why men shouldn't come in and out of it. The smell of leather, the smell of sweat, cum and fear... yours.

Faceless, guilty looking, averting their eyes, their fingers going to their wedding rings subconsciously. Flaccid cocks, disappearing back into trousers. The guy, Jim, who paid you a tenner to fuck you in the arse.

You remembered you bought your first pair of trainers with that money. The lady in the shop had told you that your uncle must think you're a "very special" nephew to get that much money for your birthday. And always there, Fitzpatrick, the ringleader – telling you that your folks were dead and that the priests and the men were your "family". Another lie.

You'd found her, a confused old lady, your birth mother, not knowing who you were. A month later a lonely crematorium where a minister who'd never known her delivered a eulogy. Did you have anything to add? No, you knew less than he did. This, just the latest gem to add to your reservoir of hate.

Fitzpatrick had been the ringleader, but O'Brien had looked on ambivalently which made him even worse in your book. He'd recognised you as he'd opened the door. The eyes of a frightened old man who knew his day of reckoning had come.

The angel of death has arrived to mete out an earthly revenge, just in case the afterlife proved to deliver the wrong verdict.

You'd even gone through the pretence of tea and biscuits. Then he'd seen the rounders bat. It was a particularly effective weapon.

He'd whimpered softly after the first few blows had turned his face into a bloody pulp. But that was enough. You'd heard him trying to splutter something through a cloud of snot, blood and phlegm.

You'd turned the gas rings on full in the kitchen and left the Paschal Candle in the church to do the rest. The ensuing explosion had blown the priest's house to smithereens and left the church a shattered hulk.

Due to the elderly nature of the dwindling congregation, the site had been levelled. A store stood there now. It opened on Sundays. O'Brien had been small fry, though. Fitzpatrick was the one you wanted. A quirk of fate, a thorough investigation by a British journalist had delivered him to you. He would need something really special. But first the girl....

# Moleshill, United Kingdom.

**B**right morning light slanted through the chinks in the curtains. Marsh flicked one eye open and looked around. It was an unfamiliar room. He pulled the duvet tighter around him and listened. There was a sound of banging from the kitchen and soon the schlurp schlurp of the coffee-maker sent the delicious smell of coffee wafting up the stairs.

He pulled on his boxer shorts and trousers and made for the bathroom. After he'd performed his ablutions he returned to the bedroom. On the side was a glass containing a Bloody Mary and two pills. Marsh had just taken a deep pull on the drink and swallowed the pills when Moore entered, wearing a dressing gown and sporting tousled hair.

"Good morning, want some breakfast?" she smiled. It all came flooding back to Marsh, a lunch of pasta and salad, a bottle of wine and then a post-dinner brandy – the smell of her hair, a kiss on the stairs. Marsh held her gaze. He looked at the empty bottle of brandy and tangled mess of clothes. He took a pull on the drink and stuttered.

"The wine, the brandy, the case notes, the kiss… we didn't, did we?" he asked.

"Well, you cheeky bastard! Actually, we finished the brandy and yes, we finished the case notes. But no, we didn't and would it have been so bad if we had? I'm no Liz Hurley but you're no Jude Law either, mister."

"Oh fuck, how do I get into these situations!" said Marsh, putting his head in his hands. She closed the distance between them and held Marsh in a tight embrace.

"Hey, you silly bastard, I'm having you on, I really like you. Don't you remember we were snogging like a couple of teenagers?

You went upstairs to go for a wee and never came back down. So, after half an hour of hearing you snore, I came back and put you to bed, that's the top and bottom of it. But if you want to pick up where we left off, then I'm ready. Once we've gone over the files, that is, and you can see what you can use."

She kissed him on the lips and went down the stairs. Still slightly bemused, Marsh followed her. In the downstairs spare bedroom which doubled up as Moore's office, an array of paper was laid out across what had once been a kitchen table. Light made a vain effort to break through the steel shutters fitted across the window. Steel bars were fixed into the brickwork inside the shutters.

"Three burglaries can make you paranoid," said Moore, taking a seat in an ageing swivel chair. "This is the main archive, but Jonathan… I err mean Peter… has copies of everything in a safe at his office. Plus, it's all scanned to microfilm and held in a fireproof safe in a bank in town," she said, acknowledging Marsh's obvious admiration for the professional way in which it had been conducted.

"A pretty slick operation," said Marsh.

"It's got to be when you take on the Catholic Church and the Australian state from your spare bedroom," she said with a sense of resignation.

She frowned and Marsh for a brief second saw some of the crow's feet and minor frown lines in her face. These, he realised were the physical scars of long nights spent researching paperwork, making international phone calls and sleepless nights clutching a cricket bat, living in fear that someone would break in and do some real harm. For Marsh, this had all seemed a bit of game; for Moore, there had been a price to pay.

"A penny for them?" said Moore.

"I was just thinking you're one hell of a woman, a real battler," said Marsh, leaning down to embrace her in a hug. They broke apart and Marsh turned to look at an iron grey filing cabinet.

"I vaguely remember that I was going to look in here today," said Marsh.

P. J. Nash

"Correct, those are the records of all the children who went through the relocation process," said Moore.

"Funny," said Marsh. We're supposed to have stopped deporting people to Australia over a century ago. And yet this crap went on well into the sixties."

"The Catholic Church's guilty little secrets had to be hidden somewhere," said Moore.

"So while the sexual revolution's happening in London, the pill, Carnaby Street, the Mini and miniskirts, something akin to bloody *Oliver Twist* is happening just up the M1 motorway," said Marsh.

"And unlike *Oliver Twist* there was no happy ending. They were promised barbecues on the beach and instead they got beaten and buggered by horny old priests," said Moore, emitting a deep sigh. "We managed to trace the archives, or what remained of them, to an antiques shop in the Cotswolds. I traced over 200 people. Out of them, thirteen had committed suicide, thirty or so have had problems with booze and drugs or both, and over half have sought treatment for mental health issues such as depression," said Moore, with a sigh.

The pair stood lost in silent thought for a few seconds. Their reverie was interrupted by the ping of an arriving email and the whir as the ancient fax machine coughed into life and began spewing out pages. Moore jogged across the room to feed some more copy paper into the machine. Marsh picked up the sheets and took a look at them. The sheets were the results of a day-long brainstorming session between several of the world's leading forensic psychiatrists. It was an impressive list of experts including the UK's leading expert who worked at the infamous Broadmoor Hospital, whose patients included Moors Murderer Ian Brady and the Yorkshire Ripper, Peter Sutcliffe. Unlike the US, which tends to execute its mass murderers, the UK had no death penalty and subsequently had the opportunity to analyse, and possibly even treat these killers.

Marsh recognised another name on the list and realised it rang a bell as one of the lecturers on the course James had attended at Quantico.

In all, there were fifteen pages. Marsh went across to the filing cabinet and picked out an armful of files. Each one was a buff manila folder with some typed sheets inside and pictures of the individual as a boy, and, if they had been found, updated shots of them as an adult. It also contained copies of their original files and transcripts of interviews Moore had carried out.

"I'm going to smoke a cigar in the garden and try and see if any of these guys match the profile our team of headshrinkers has come up with," said Marsh.

"Okay, I'll take a pile and see what I can come up with, too," said Moore.

It didn't escape either of their attentions, the manner in which they quickly divided their tasks and got on with it. Both were seasoned journalists and it was instinctive for them to seek out a corner and quietly get to work. Marsh took his pile of documents out into the garden, nipped the end off a Romeo Y Julieta and struck a match, careful to let the head burn itself off before applying the flame. He held up the match and rolled the cigar in the flame. Dropping the match into an ashtray he took a pull on the cigar and tasted the smoke.

His mind began to clear and the previous night's events came back to him. Moore had told him about the mysterious lawyer who had introduced himself as "Jonathan Swift". It turned out he was called Peter Chilvers, a senior partner at Chilvers Street & Wilde – a pre-eminent law firm in Birmingham.

He was number seventy-two in the files.

To all intents and purposes, Chilvers was a fifty-something man who had made it. He was handsome, wealthy and married with three children. Despite this, he still found himself risking ruin by seeking out rough sex with rent boys at Birmingham's Digbeth Coach Station at least twice a month.

Chilvers had been an altar boy in a Birmingham parish when he had caught the attentions of a certain Father Neil Fitzpatrick. Hundreds of hours of the best therapists money could buy had only delivered the same result. Fitzpatrick had fucked him sexually and he could only achieve sexual gratification in the way he'd been abused. So when he heard of Moore's one-woman campaign he decided to back her. This had first taken the form of a sports bag containing £30,000 in untraceable banknotes.

A few months later, when it became apparent that Moore could not cope with the volume of work, Chilvers set up a small law firm with a brass plate address in London. Two young lawyers were employed through an intermediary to work on the project under the guidance of Moore and some discreet legal advice from Chilvers.

The lawyers had shuttled back and forth between the UK and Australia interviewing victims and asking awkward questions in churches, houses and retirement homes in both countries. They had also brought their legal expertise to bear, obtaining records from children's homes and churches from a period dating back from the early 1950s to the 1980s. Moore had also retained the services of a former colleague at her newspaper, Graham Taylor.

A nicotine-stained newshound of the old school, Taylor had acted in the main as a private investigator, going to places where a suit and a law degree did not open doors.

Once Moore had been burgled the third time and it became obvious that the play had turned dirty and that the proverbial gloves were off, she had used Taylor to liberate documents which no amount of lawyer's letters written on creamy headed notepaper would yield forth.

Taylor's human touch had come in handy, too. Some of the victims were in a bad way, due to years of boozing or pills. They had been much more forthcoming to the wizened street fighter, who recorded their recollection in shorthand on a pad, a cigarette dangling from the corner of his mouth and a glass of cheap scotch within easy reach. He got people to open up like this in a way no law school graduate with a suit and a digital recorder could have done. On more than a few occasions Taylor had slept on the sofa at Moore's house. She had begun to associate the smell of cigarettes and whisky with a sense of security.

Marsh riffled the pages of the reports and pulled out a few, selecting them via names he liked from various areas of his life. This was the system he used when he made an infrequent visit to the horse races. Curtis, the same name as the lead singer of Joy Division; Marr, the genius guitar player from the Smiths; Havilland, now that stood out ... De Havilland, an aircraft manufacturer.

A shiver ran down Marsh's spine, followed by a surge of adrenaline. Marsh didn't know how he knew. This was their man… He put his cigar down in the ashtray and raced for the phone.

\*\*\*

Derek Sebastian Havilland: born October 19th 1950, Kidderminster, Worcestershire, England. Father: John Havilland, full-time alcoholic and sometime construction labourer. Mother: Jane Havilland, full-time beaten wife and housekeeper.

In 1954, three months behind with the rent and the ground frozen – meaning no work – John, in a moment of sobriety, talks to the parish priest who had "just popped by" to see Jane because she hadn't attended church.

The three-inch gash in her left cheek was caused by flying glass; when returning from the pub, John had kicked the door in. Foundation and a scarf couldn't keep this one hidden. There had been talk after mass amongst the men. So sometimes "her indoors" deserved a slap if she got lippy, but leaving her looking like a punch bag was just not done. Maybe it was time for a taste of his own medicine? So, acting peacemaker, the priest had gone for a quiet word.

"Australia," said John incredulously, as he sat, unshaven, at the kitchen table, drinking sherry from a chipped teacup. Father O'Hanlon had suggested Jane Havilland take the "wee man" down to the swings. John saw that his options were limited. Take the envelope with a donation from the parish and get on the boat; or take a hiding and end up homeless. On 25th February 1954 the family set sail from Southampton on a foggy day.

P. J. Nash

John never made it. A game of cards with some sailors – a dispute over a few pounds – a punch, a flash of steel – John Havilland lying on a dirty steel floor – blood pumping from his carotid artery.

It wasn't so much grief that Jane felt but a loss of how to explain her life without the domineering bully. She locked herself in her cabin, cut her wrists and so ended her life.

The sailor had acted in self-defence, the captain's word at sea was law. No refrigeration for two bodies, so a double burial at sea, the events typed up on two sheets of foolscap, arriving with little Derek at St Columbus' home for orphans.

The abuse had started when they asked you to strip naked for a lice bath. It had carried pretty much on that way for eleven years, then there'd been relief – a scholarship to a Melbourne sixth form.

You'd only got so clever by disseminating your fear and diverting yourself through reading, staying up into the early hours, too terrified of what might come in the night.

Apart from the Elliot Butler incident. He'd thought, seeing as you were the priest's plaything, you were fair game for anyone. He waited till lights out, came across and grabbed your cock. You had a book in your hands, a big old leather-bound edition of Dickens. You caught Butler a glancing blow with it and knocked him to the floor. You went over to him, making sure the brass corners were facing him and brought the tome down on his face. Again and again. You were breathless after that. You remembered the only worry you had was that the book might be damaged and you would be in trouble. And also a sense of omnipotence and power which you had never felt before. But you knew you would need to feel it again.

Fitzpatrick discovered the body. The next day all the boys had been assembled in the hall. You were told that Butler had stolen away in the night. Stumbling through the bush he'd made it to a road only to be hit by a truck. The Requiem mass was held the following day.

Swanston Academy, academic success and your first attention from girls. They liked your awkwardness and the more you tried to ignore them, the keener they got. One in particular, Rita, pretty, thin and totally into you. You'd done your best to avoid her, but she engineered a situation where you got to be together. A philosophy seminar, Descartes. She came back to the crummy studio apartment you had rented on your bursary.

You'd hit the books, then she asked for a drink. You went to the fridge to get a can of Coke. When you came back she had her t-shirt off.

"Come over and sit down," she'd said. You'd just stood, mouth agape. "Cat got your tongue?" she asked. She'd slid her hands onto your crotch and began stroking it.

You'd moved away, she'd followed. "What's up, you gay or something?"

The upward cut of the heel of your right hand snapped her neck. With a slight gurgle she dropped to the floor. The fear that had welled up in you when she touched you dissipated instantly. The martial arts training had paid off. You were on the seventh floor. You'd packed a holdall, pushed her off the balcony and went to Adelaide for a week.

The inquest returned a verdict of "death by misadventure". Your passion for killing had begun. A degree, a PhD, an academic career, and Deborah... to whom you'd lost your virginity and your heart.

# Hancock mansion, Boxwood, Northern Territory.

Deborah Hancock sucked on her cigarette as if her life depended on it, drawing in the smoke as if it possessed some life-giving properties. She sat on a reproduction Victorian chaise longue, one hand picking absent-mindedly at the hem of her cashmere cardigan.

James sat on a leather sofa holding a pen in one hand, a reporter's notebook open on his lap. He'd made a few symbolic doodles which were reminiscent of Pitman shorthand; he'd learned it during his journalism course, back before he joined the thin blue line. In fact, it was the afternoons spent in magistrates and Crown Courts around the industrial English Midlands that had helped him decide he'd like to do something proactive to stop the hoodlums that clogged up the court system, rather than just relaying the lurid details of horrific crimes to scare the great British public over their cornflakes.

"Can I get you some coffee?" asked Hancock, with a clink of jewellery. James nodded and was just about to say yes, but Hancock pushed an intercom button and spoke to an unseen person.

James imagined a bell ringing in some kitchen below the stairs. On pulling the rope bell pull at the porch of the Hancock mansion, a line from a Raymond Chandler novel had entered into James' mind about "calling on four million dollars".

"It'll be here in a jiffy," said Hancock. Although she was into her sixties, Hancock was a good-looking woman who exuded a sense of power and sexual allure. James thought she reminded him of Helen Mirren. But snakes alive, you'd have to have skin like a rhinoceros, to be married to Terry Hancock for nigh on thirty years, an attractive, intelligent woman to boot.

A clinking of porcelain ended the silence. A thirty-something Filipino woman, dressed in a smart business suit, brought in a tray. The china was Royal Worcester, the coffee was Columbian, and James had a detective's nose for such things. The younger woman poured the coffee.

"Milk?" she asked.

"Yes, please. Just a splash," said James, slowly and deliberately.

"Miss Cheung speaks perfectly good English. She did an MBA at Warwick University," snapped Hancock, giving James a scolded look.

"No offence taken," smiled the young woman. "Nikki Cheung, good to meet you," she said extending her hand. "Mrs Hancock's a little over-sensitive on the issue of my nationality," said Cheung. "Her husband's friends can be a little stereotypical at times."

"Racist bastards, you mean?" asked James.

"Well, I wouldn't use quite those words, but the sentiment is correct," Cheung replied, with a wry smile. She made a sort of semi-bow and left without further ado.

James reached for his coffee. Discreetly tucked under his saucer was Cheung's business card. He palmed it as he picked up the cup and saucer. He took a sip, it was good and it was hot.

"So, Mrs Hancock, let's talk about that night and just who was coming to see you, and why your husband was so keen for this information," said James.

"I could spend all day here telling you what my husband's up to and all the little tramps and whores he's been with to shit on his wedding vows. But if I do, the Valium will probably put me out before I've got past our supposed honeymoon. So I'll cut a long story short. He's the only man I ever loved and still do. Two words are all you need, Derek Havilland."

# Bristol, United Kingdom.

Geoff Wilmott was eating his lunch and watching *Look West*, the regional news programme for Bristol and the South-West. He had been a fitter at Avon Caravans for three years; his routine was to watch the BBC lunch time news and then *Look West*, and he liked Lisa Tamil, the weather girl. In hindsight he would come to realise that if it hadn't been for this he would never have made the link.

He was tucking into his last round of corned beef and tomato when the item came on the television. "And finally, Australian Police are appealing for further information from tourists from the UK who might have visited the Northern Territory, following the abduction of British girl Jenny Somerville who hails from the Midlands, but whose parents now live here in Bristol. Last night Northern Territory Police released footage of the moments just before Jenny Somerville was abducted and her boyfriend Edgar Wallace was fatally stabbed," the newscaster said. The footage cut to some grainy CCTV footage of a van. Then the images were slowed down and enhanced. Wilmott spat out his sandwich.

"Bugger me, it's one of ours," he exclaimed.

His boss, Geoff Taylor, ducked to avoid a spray of tomato and partially chewed corned beef. "What, you mean the van?" he asked.

"Yes, do you remember, the lecturer type – leather elbow patches, pipe going like a bloody chimney," replied Wilmott.

"Old git, was he?" asked Taylor.

"Not really, he was probably fifty-odd, but dressed older; you know, cords and brogues," said Wilmott.

"I think I know who you mean," replied Taylor.

"You should do, you were drooling all over his daughter," replied Wilmott.

"The one in the denim shorts was his *daughter*? I thought he was a randy old sod who'd got lucky." Geoff laughed and walked into the glass-fronted office, sat down at his desk and tapped on the keyboard. "Havilland," he shouted out to Wilmott over the din of woodworking machinery.

"Better get on the blower, pronto," said Wilmott, who was now tucking into a pickled egg.

"Yeah, you're right, and maybe it explains why he wanted those compartments adding. Creepy, when you think about it… Hello Avon and Somerset Police? I have some information that might help you."

# Our Lady of the Angels Church, Tarmie, Northern Territory.

Father Neil Fitzpatrick was an embezzler and sycophant. These were his good points. He was also a serial predatory paedophile.

Unlike others possessed of this affliction he had not locked it in a box in the dark recesses of his consciousness, only for it to occasionally break out like a chimera which could not be tamed, but rather embraced it and pursued it to the limits of its inevitable depravity.

Despite this pederastic zeal, he presented a public countenance of an affable, white-haired elderly priest, serving out his retirement in a parish where nothing much happened. No one would have guessed this was the man who had single-handedly run a campaign of terror, stalking the corridors, immersing himself in the most depraved of acts.

He had also cynically sold the "rights" to abuse boys to other paedophiles who had to pay for their privileges that Fitzpatrick had taken as his right.

He took mass once a day in the week and twice on Saturdays and Sundays, giving middle-of-the-road sermons to his dwindling flock of elderly parishioners. Every so often one would die and Father Fitzpatrick would conduct the Requiem mass and, more often than not, received a bequest from their will. This he put to good use in going on a break to somewhere like Thailand, or more recently Myanmar, where paedophile sex tourism was burgeoning. It had become a hotspot after the Royal Thai Police had finally begun to get a grip on the vile trade in molestation of young people which had gone unhindered for so many years. Some of these funds had also gone into a top-of-the-range computer allowing Fitzpatrick to indulge in his vile predilections from the anonymity of cyberspace. Despite his advanced years the elderly priest had not been slow in seeing the advantages of the internet.

A series of external hard drives hidden around the house contained his collection. His main computer was whiter than white. Despite the best efforts of law enforcement agencies throughout the world, paedophiles have been particularly adroit at staying one step ahead of the game. Plus, Fitzpatrick took the phlegmatic view that he was a 76-year-old priest. Even if he got caught red-handed he'd get a couple of years in an open prison.

His view was just about to change dramatically.

# Unknown location, Northern Territory.

Jenny Somerville lay still, playing possum, lying on the mattress.

She'd done this the last three times that her captor had been down to her basement cell. From the glances she'd managed to get, she had got the idea that there were probably two of them. They both wore boiler suits, gloves and comedy rubber masks. Tony Blair had brought her dinner the previous evening; George Bush had brought her breakfast this morning.

Despite their similar disguises, she had worked out that one was slighter than the other and the larger one always smelt like pipe tobacco, similar to her favourite uncle, John. The smaller one also took more care to place her food on a tray off the floor, rather just pushing it through the door. She – Jenny presumed it was a she – also made better food.

From a quick glance she saw it was the pipe man. He opened the door with a tray in his hand, something he'd not done before. He seemed to be distracted, somehow. He dropped the keys. She saw her chance and took it. She sprang to her feet. He span round to face her, not quite sure what her intentions were. In a fraction of a second a flash hit him and he was blinded.

Jenny had shone into his eyes the laser light from a pointer she had had in her jeans pocket the day she was abducted.

He groaned and his hands went to his eyes.

She sprang across the room and kneed him in the crotch. He groaned even louder and doubled over in pain. She picked up the bottle she had adapted and squeezed it, a jet of piss hitting him square in the face and stinging his eyes. Her right hand came back and she plunged a fountain pen into his leg, once, twice, three times. Blood poured from his leg and he collapsed in a heap.

She picked up the keys and began to fiddle with them. Luck was with her. She opened the big padlock that had held the chain to the wall, and, hands and legs still chained together, went to make out of the room.

He was getting to his knees; she picked up the padlock and swung it into his face, his nose cracking, another groan and a spurt of blood from behind the mask. He sank back down to the floor.

She picked her way out through the open door and out into the dank corridor. Holding the bloodied padlock aloft to use as a weapon, she made her way up the stairs. There was no sound apart from the odd drip, drip of water from higher up the stairway. She slowly made her way up them to where shards of light were poking through a partially opened door. She got there and tugged on it. It was heavy, but she leant her weight on it and it creaked open.

Daylight flooded in and hurt her eyes. The door was one like she'd see in war films, heavy, made of steel and several inches thick. Surging with adrenaline and unsteady on her feet, she staggered through clumps of spinifex, looking to gain some kind of direction and also to put distance between her and her abductor. Her escape had come off and now she didn't want to squander the opportunity.

She had formulated the plan and it had gone swimmingly.

It was the drink she recognised that was spiked with tranquillisers. She'd not drunken a drop in two days and had put the devious mixture straight into the piss bucket. It had left her desperately thirsty, but she had managed to get some untainted water by catching drops from the ceiling on a plate. She staggered on into the bush, slightly delirious.

Then a hand grabbed her from behind.

# Havilland house, Boxwood, Northern Territory.

The raid on Havilland's address was put together in more of a hurry than James or Sandersen would have liked, but both agreed time was of the essence. There was nothing to say he, or they, as it now seemed to be, would keep to a strict timetable. The time for profiling was over; the time for action was here. James strapped on his Kevlar vest as the unmarked van made for the rendezvous point, a street away from the one-storey house which had been identified from Avon Caravans' customer database, and set the ball rolling.

The assault team would be a dozen cops in plain clothes; six taking the front, six taking the back. James pushed a clip into his Beretta 9mm pistol and racked a round into the chamber. His arm hurt like a bastard, and a light sweat was on his brow. His throat tasted of bile, the tangible taste of fear. The last time he'd been on a raid he had been shot. No wonder he was a little nervous. Added to which, none of the men and women in the team with him had worked with him before.

The van drew up to a halt and the team exited from a side door. Guns drawn, they jogged at an easy lope down an alley which ran down the side of the target house. Further down the street, police cars were pulling up and forming road blocks. Uniform cops in full body armour carrying shotguns and M16s were forming a perimeter.

James and the others squeezed through a gap in the fence and ran across the lawn. The largest cop had a sledgehammer. James and another cop unhooked grenades from their tactical vests and pulled the pins. Simultaneously, they bowled them over-arm through two different windows. There was a tinkling of glass followed by a series of flashes and bangs as the grenades exploded. The large cop swung the hammer and the front door splintered to matchwood and swung in. James rushed into the gap, gun up, screaming, "Police! Stay where you are."

Crashes and bangs followed from the rear as the other team smashed their way in. As agreed, they were to only break in the rear door and secure the first room to prevent any friendly-fire incidents. James and the others took the rooms in pairs, kicking in doors and securing them.

They were all empty. The bird – or birds – had flown.

"Fuck!" shouted James, as his adrenaline drained away and a sense of despondency took over. He tore off his vest and sat down on the lawn of the house.

A uniform cop offered him a cigarette which he was quick to take. He drew on it and took a deep breath, his heartbeat returning to normal. A convoy of cars and vans drew up; the forensic boys. Sandersen got out of one of them, made her way over to James and embraced him.

"We fucking missed him," said James.

"I know, but tearing out our hair isn't going to save the girl, is it?" she said. "We've got to get in there and find out what we can. It was a slim chance he'd have her tied up in the living room while he did his ironing, wasn't it?" she said, stroking James' hair.

This raised a smile from him. "Yeah, I suppose you're right."

"Let's get in there and see what makes him tick," said Sandersen, walking towards the house.

# Former RAAF Churchill, Boxwood, Northern Territory.

John "Walkabout" Smith had caught Jenny Somerville as she fell. He was on the site of the disused airfield picking up junk metal and putting it in the back of his pickup. He'd heard a noise behind him and seen her stagger out of the clump of bushes.

He'd caught her and even before he'd straightened her up, he knew she was the missing girl. Instantly, he felt the thrill of discovery and then a secondary feeling of trepidation. If he drove her to the hospital in Boxwood he'd be up before the cops and have to answer lots of awkward questions. For one, why he was on the site anyway? He wasn't getting fitted up by the racist cops.

He took another course of action. He gave the girl a decent drink of water and got her to eat a couple of snack bars, high in glucose, that he kept for emergencies. He drove to the outskirts of Boxwood, leant the delirious girl against a phone booth, wrapped her in a blanket, and put a bottle of water by her side. Then he rang the cops from the phone box and high-tailed it out of there.

Within eight minutes uniform cops and an ambulance were on the scene and Jenny was safe once again.

The little bitch, she'd got you good. How could you have been so careless? She'd jumped you, plain and simple.

Luckily, Alison had gotten back from shopping before you had bled to death on the floor. Stabbed with a fountain pen, it bloody hurt. Now she'd gotten away, but you couldn't stick around to find her. She might live, she might die, and the real dingoes might get her. Either way she knew bugger all, really. But she was the least of your worries.

The van had probably been identified now; it was pretty much only a matter of time.

Get Alison on the plane and you go and finish the last piece of business. If the cops get in your way, you'd use the gun, no worries.

What's a cop or two on the pile after this many bodies and this long a time?

# Havilland house, Boxwood, Northern Territory.

The one-storey house had not yielded much and the surroundings were pretty much in keeping with the house of a middle-aged academic. This was not news to seasoned professionals like Sandersen and James who were quite used to the juxtaposition of apparent normal domesticity and extreme evil.

Crime writers and film directors like to focus on the idea of photographs of victims pinned to the walls and secret torture chambers. The truth was more pedestrian. Victims were strangled with tea towels and buried in shallow graves in woods. If they were held captive, they were held captive in dingy flats or secluded industrial units.

James and Sandersen started on Havilland's study. It was full of books on a multitude of subjects. Now wearing forensic suits and gloves, the pair combed through the drawers of his desks and looked for clues. James' eyes strayed to a book he recognised from the past. A Catholic diocesan directory. It pricked his attention and he picked it up.

"What are you thinking?" asked Sandersen.

"I'm not sure, but I think there's something here, it stands out somehow? It doesn't fit in. It's a darn sight newer than all the others and it's not been here long," said James.

"I can see it's new, but how can you tell it's not been here for long?" said Sandersen.

"It doesn't stink of pipe smoke," said James, with a smile.

Then something happened they didn't expect. The telephone on the desk rang. The pair looked at it for a few seconds.

"You better answer it," said Sandersen. James tentatively picked it up.

"Hello?" he said.

"James, it's Marsh here. I've got news for you."

"How did you get this number?" asked James."

"Havilland emailed a full confession to me, Sandersen and all the British papers, it's gonna cause a shit-storm here and in Oz too."

"Fuck me, when did you get it?" exclaimed James.

"About ten minutes ago. It's massive, but the phone number was at the bottom. I thought I'd give him a bell," said Marsh.

"Ever the journo. I'm afraid he can't come to the phone at the moment," quipped James. "Why would Havilland have a new copy of a diocesan directory here in his study? It stands out like a sore thumb amongst all this sociology and Marxist stuff."

"Look for a Father Neil Fitzpatrick," said Marsh.

"What's the link?" asked James.

"He was the ringleader of the paedophile priests at the home where Havilland was resident for three years. We found his file in the archives here. He abused boys here in the UK and they got him out of the way by sending him to Oz," said Marsh.

"Found him," said Sandersen.

"Two priests that were possibly involved in the abuse have both died in the last two years," said Marsh.

"Murdered?" asked James.

"It seems accidental, a car accident and a gas explosion: they could both have been staged, but it seems more than mere coincidence, don't you think?" said Marsh.

"Agreed. We gotta go, Father Fitzpatrick is parish priest at Our Lady of the Angels in Tarmie," said James. "Thanks for the link. We'll call you back once we've got the old guy secure."

"Don't make too much of an effort: he's a grade-A bastard," said Marsh.

"Duty and all that. Sorry, can't make moral decisions," said James, putting down the phone.

Sandersen had already got three other detectives mobilised and they jumped into one car. James had the tactical radio in his hands as they sped off, Sandersen driving at top speed.

# Our Lady of the Angels Church, Tarmie, Northern Territory.

Father Neil Fitzpatrick hadn't even considered that it was possible to feel this much pain and not pass out or die.

He had learned by this time that either there was no God, or if there was, his prayers were falling on deaf ears. The rush of adrenaline that hit him after the initial battering had worn off and now the pain had set in.

He'd lost consciousness at one point but had been revived after being dunked, head first, into the font. He had to admit to himself, he'd not thought this would happen. None of them would come looking for him.

His confidence in his ability to outclass his victims and to manipulate them had been his weakness. He would never have opened the door if it had been a man. But the girl had looked so vulnerable via the CCTV screen. That was until she head-butted him, breaking his nose, and then shattered both of his kneecaps with a rounders bat. There had been worse to come.

He looked down at the pool of blood which dripped from his crotch. He knew death was inevitable but only his torturer knew how long would elapse between the dying embers of his life and the eternal damnation that he thought awaited him.

\*\*\*

By the time the car driven by Sandersen screeched to a halt outside the church, a couple of uniform cars had parked themselves across either end of the quietly prosperous street. Guns drawn, they covered the exits and entrances without making an effort to storm the building. James and Sandersen, both clad in bulletproof vests, and James with his gun drawn, made their way over to the ad hoc cordon.

"Who's in charge here?" James asked.

A constable nodded to a senior sergeant busy loading Magnum shells into his pump-action shotgun.

"Alright, sarge, is he definitely in there?" asked James.

"You the cavalry?" he asked.

"Suppose so," said James.

"We're pretty sure he's in there; the housekeeper came in the back door with some shopping. She heard screams from the church, took a look through a side door and saw a guy whacking the old priest with some sort of bat. She did the right thing and got the hell out. She seems to think there's a young girl in there, possibly a hostage. I was told to secure the perimeter, till you came."

"Righty-ho, you've done well so far. Just make sure the perimeter is as tight as a gnat's chuff. I'm gonna give him a call and see what he wants," said James.

"Sounds like a plan," said the fat sergeant. "You think he's got a gun?"

"I doubt it, but either way he's not going to let anyone in carrying one, is he?" replied James.

James dialled the number of the presbytery. The fat cop watched, intrigued.

*** 

The telephone's ring echoed through the almost empty church. What remained of Father Neil Fitzpatrick was slumped on the altar, bleeding and wheezing through a broken nose and a throat full of blood. His efforts to clear his throat failed as many of the bones in his hand were broken. Havilland had smashed them with the base of a heavy brass crucifix.

Seated on pews a few feet away were Havilland and Alison. Havilland was sweating from his exertions and blood was spattered over his shirt. Alison cradled the rounders bat, which was covered in gore.

"I suppose I'd better answer, hadn't I?" he said.

He moved across the altar, through into the vestry and picked up the receiver of an aged telephone.

"Hello," said Havilland.

"Lawrence James, lead investigator here. I believe you are Mr Havilland?"

"That's correct, Mr James. What can I do for you?" he said, nonchalantly.

"Well, ideally, I'd like you to come out of the church with your hands where we can see them and lie face down on the ground in a spread-eagle position," said James, calmly.

"What if I don't?"

"Well, several of my heavily armed colleagues will enter the church and blow you apart with shotguns, I suppose," said James.

"Something tells me you're not a trained negotiator, Mr James," Havilland replied with a small laugh.

"I'm not negotiating, I'm just stating the facts, Mr Havilland."

"Well, maybe if I told you I had a young female here as hostage, does that change the rules of the game? You've got the guns, I've got the girl. Checkmate, it would seem, Mr James," said Havilland with obvious relish.

"I'm not sure if its checkmate, but you seem to have a couple of aces up your sleeve, admittedly, Mr Havilland."

"Here's the deal: you come up to the front of the church unarmed and alone. Come into the church and I'll send out the girl. Sound okay?" said Havilland.

"Sounds about the best we can agree on," said James.

"Look forward to seeing you," said Havilland, putting down the phone.

"You going in?" said the fat sergeant.

"Seems that way," said James, once more taking off his bulletproof vest, and taking off his shoulder holster and offering both to the other cop. Then he crossed the road, arms out beside him and moved towards the church. He entered, his footsteps echoing on the marble floor. He saw the dying priest first, in a crumpled heap, a trail of blood leading to the altar where he'd been dragged. Then he saw the gun, a Luger, a real antique, but a real enough killer none the less.

Havilland was about fiftyish, his brown hair greying at the temples, fit looking enough for an academic. He swayed on the balls of his feet, the gun trained on James' heart. While he didn't look like a natural marksman, James knew he'd have no problem pulling the trigger.

"Ah, Mr James, I presume," said Havilland sarcastically, his blue eyes flashing. "Take a seat next to our young hostage." He pointed to the pew where a young woman, small, but pretty and with dark hair, was seated, a rope round her hands and her legs also tied. She gave James a wry smile as if to say, *He got you, too?*

James sat down on the pew. Havilland swung the gun to cover James.

"Sweet little popgun you got there," said James.

"It's a family heirloom, the only thing that the old man passed onto me. He won it off a Filipino seaman, who slit his throat. They tossed my mum and dad in the sea. Then I went to a home for boys where I got rogered by dirty old fuckers like him over there," said Havilland, his face distorted in a mask of hatred. "Well, anyway, the day I left, an old nun shuffles over to me and gives me this. There were even two clips with it. I've fired a couple off just to make sure the old girl works. There's something about the smell of cordite… it's like the antithesis of incense, it's the cleansing flame," said Havilland.

James sensed that he was psyching himself up to do something. Havilland made towards the dying priest.

"I think it's time for his last rites, what do you think?" asked Havilland. He raised the gun.

James realised he only had a fraction of a second. He leapt to his feet, but his weakened arm let him down at the critical moment. He fell awkwardly, rolled and looked up just as Havilland fired twice into the priest's forehead. A spray of pink mist flew from his head.

James sprang forward to catch Havilland before he could turn and fire. In the same instant a flash came into his peripheral vision, followed by a searing pain. Letting out a banshee-like howl he carried on over and knocked Havilland sprawling. He pinned Havilland's gun arm down, the pistol skittered across the floor and out of both of their reaches.

James got in a couple of punches into Havilland's face. He seemed impervious. A shadow flickered across them and James felt a rush of air as a blade swished by narrowly missing him. It was the girl, wielding a combat knife, her eyes wild with anger.

James, deciding she posed the most immediate threat, rolled off Havilland. He dodged as she tried to stab him in the chest. Catching her overextended, he slammed the heel of his hand into to the girl's face. Her nose smashed and her head snapped back, she dropped the knife and fell to the floor, blood streaming from her face. James stood dazed for a second too long. Havilland smashed the butt of the gun into the back of his head. He saw stars literally and fell to the hard stone floor. Luckily, he fell on his bad arm, which broke his fall. He went to roll over, but Havilland's foot stomped onto his chest.

"I would have let you go if you hadn't hit my girl," said Havilland raising the Luger. "If you'd let me do the priest I'd have let you have the gun. I know when enough's enough," said Havilland, breathing heavily.

"You forgot when to stop years ago, Havilland," said James.

"What the fuck would you know?" said Havilland, raising the gun. "You should have stayed in England, copper," said Havilland, going to squeeze the trigger.

But James had kept him talking just long enough. He had moved his booted foot round to the back of Havilland's leg. With a superhuman effort he pulled himself forward and hooked Havilland's leg, knocking him off balance. The gun fired harmlessly into the ceiling. At the same instant James' arm flashed up and came across Havilland's throat. He staggered backwards clutching his throat and made a horrendous gurgling noise as dark gouts of blood spouted from his throat.

James stood over him, his hands at his side. In the left one a credit card – glued to the rear of it, a Stanley knife blade shone brightly, a sheen of blood on it. The silence was shattered as six uniform cops, guns up, ran into the church, shouting, "Police, stay where you are."

"Watch that bitch, she's his daughter," said James.

One of the cops who'd followed the cops with guns, had a baton drawn and mace in the other hand. Pumped up on adrenaline he sprayed her in the face and beat her about the body with the baton. She screamed in pain. Two other cops pulled him off.

It was at that moment that James put his hand down to his side and felt the warm dampness of his own blood and collapsed into unconsciousness.

# Chandler Hospital, Chandler, Northern Territory.

Sandersen walked over to James' hospital bed. He was propped up on pillows. A few bruises showed on his face. Underneath the covers he had twenty-three stitches running up his left side where Alison's knife had struck home. He'd lost six pints of blood and been in surgery for a couple of hours. But he was safe enough. James looked up from his bed.

"Morning, how are you feeling?" she said.

"Not too bad," he said. "So what's happened?"

"Havilland got zipped up in a rubber bag, so did the priest. Alison has been sectioned and taken to the Monrovia Clinic in Darwin. They're holding her in the psychiatric ward under heavy sedation. I'm going to give her a few days to calm down, and a colleague and I will assess her. It's unlikely she'll go to trial," said Sandersen.

"Jenny Somerville?" James asked.

"She was found by a phone box, dehydrated but otherwise unharmed."

"That's great," said James, and drifted off into a drug-induced sleep.

# EPILOGUE

Lawrence James made a full recovery from his wounds. Later that year, he left the Victoria Police and started a psychological crime consultancy with Sandersen, based in Melbourne.

Johnson, Collins and Toohey also left the force and joined James' business as freelance investigators.

Alison Havilland was sentenced to be detained at Her Majesty's Pleasure, or, in plain language, to be held for an indeterminate time until she was either deemed to be cured or fit to be put on trial. She was held at a secure mental hospital.

Sandersen wrote a best-selling book profiling Havilland and the back-story of his life.

Marsh stayed together with Moore and flitted back between Australia and the UK. With the help of the now dry Baz Twomlow, he co-authored a book on the activities of The Brotherhood. It caused a sensation in the Northern Territory and soon the authorities launched a wide-scale investigation into Terry Hancock and his cohorts. Hancock was forced to resign from the boards of all the companies he worked for.

Overcome by guilt for not revealing the existence of Alison, Deborah Hancock committed suicide, taking an overdose of Valium.

The whereabout of Cyrus Bain remain unknown.

# Dark Angel

**By P.J Nash**
Coming Spring 2018

# Prologue

## Prague, Czech Republic

Jana Markova was tired from her cleaning job as she entered the metro carriage at Nové Butovice. She had made her way through the windswept canyons of the austere communist-era tower blocks to the underground station and entered the carriage without really looking.

The carriage doors hissed shut and the train cannoned back into the subterranean network. She sat down and began searching for her phone which had fallen into the bottom of her capacious handbag. Managing to get hold of the phone she pulled it out and turned it over to look at the screen. Suddenly the train braked sharply. The phone shot from her hands and skittered down the centre aisle of the carriage.

She turned to look for it, but instead saw him. Or it. A scream formed in her throat, but then died. She began to hyperventilate, staggered to the doors and hit the emergency stop button…

Lightning Source UK Ltd.
Milton Keynes UK
UKOW01f2357280218
318679UK00001B/84/P